THE LINGERLINGS

Laura Wacha

Good Riddance Books

With Gratitude

To those who didn't say,

"Enough already"

Book One – There And Then

1 Maps

Trudy smiled, glancing in the rear-view mirror at the satisfying reflection of the green handles flapping in the bed of her pickup truck. She had finally remembered to bring all of those reusable shopping bags with her on the long drive to the grocery store. So often she had forgotten, driving away from the five acres of New Mexico desert that she shared with her husband and two teenaged kids and leaving the pile of bags on the counter or sitting right beside the front door. She would sometimes remember them when she was partway to town, usually on the

1

highway that ran past an old but still functioning dairy that the kids had long ago dubbed the "Stinky Milkman Dairy." The powerful odor would spark Trudy's olfactory nerves, awakening some part of her memory banks, and an image of the green bags and where they were located would appear in her brain. Unfortunately, being near the dairy also put her way too far from home to turn back. "It just wouldn't be very conscientious to use all that gas to drive back," she thought, "not to mention the wear and tear on the springs and shocks of the pickup." No, she couldn't see buying more bags at the store either, even though the family was flush with money since her husband became the premier expert on chupacabras. It just wasn't in Trudy's nature to spend unnecessarily. "Save the planet," she thought, "but save for college, too!"

She turned off the highway at the Bernardo exit and rattled her old truck down the dirt road toward home. The condition of the road varied with the changing of the seasons and today it was a bit muddy, owing to last night's rain. Slipping a bit, the truck came over the little ridge that laid about two and a half miles from I-25 and afforded a view of their old mobile home in the distance, surrounded by acres and acres of comforting nothingness. Her old pals from her Art College days thought she was crazy, taking leave of the city and all of its attractions and amenities and marrying a zoologist (of all things) and moving back out to the desert. "What? No museums? No restaurants? No bookstores?" they would exclaim. Plus,

Bernardo wasn't even the picturesque Georgia O'Keefe kind of desert full of painted rock canyons, but rather the tough dry desert of rattlesnakes and sagebrush and skinny, free roaming cattle. For Trudy it was exactly that part of the "edge of nowhere" New Mexico that felt just right. She loved the big clear blue skies, the wide open spaces, and the scant population. She also loved the fact that the people she met there had real jobs that she could get her head around, like tractor mechanic, dairy farmer, school teacher, fence welder. Although she had spent some five years in Manhattan, she never could understand what a Financial Reporting Manager did all day and why anyone would want to be a graphic artist in their employ. Trudy's husband, Frank, worked at the zoo up in Albuquerque and that was something she could get her head around too. Dr. Mater was a zoologist dedicated to the care, feeding and breeding of some of the world's most unusual and endangered creatures. "Nice," she thought.

Trudy took a left turn, sending the truck down the dirt track that served as their driveway, and smiled at the sight of not only an already open gate, but of two pickup trucks parked in the yard: Frank's little old maroon one and Marsha's new little yellow one, side by side. Everybody home, most likely, since Shawn still wasn't old enough for legal driving and had to rely on the licenses of others. Trudy parked her truck beside Frank's and grabbed a couple of the green bags full of groceries and sundries and headed for the steps of the mobile home. She had to navigate the low rattlesnake fence around the house, put

3

there when the kids were toddlers, and two mud puddles, strange desert remnants from that overnight rainstorm. Opening the front door, Trudy called out, "Yo, any able bodies home? *Your* Mom could use some help unloading *your* food from the truck!" She looked at the three backs bent over the kitchen table. The usual Formica was covered with a layer of papers, as though the kids were preparing for some sort of messy art project or science experiment. Trudy was about to tell them to move their mess to the picnic table outside when she noticed that the papers covering her usual grocery unloading spot were topographical maps and not old newspapers.

"Mom, you're home!" grinned Marsha, happy to see her mother.

"With food!" joined in Shawn, always happy to see breakfast or lunch or dinner.

"And if you want to eat, my dear Shawn, you'll traipse out to the truck and help unload the groceries." She paused, shifting her gaze to her husband, and addressed him perfunctorily. "Frank, there's some water to bring in, too," she told him. The quality of the Mater family's well water had been tested a couple of times and the result had always been that the water was "okay" to drink. "After a few days of diarrhea, you'll get used to it," the man had said. So water was hauled in five gallon jugs from a coin-operated machine in town. Only one dollar if the thing didn't eat your quarters.

"Well, hello to you, too, Trudy!" laughed Frank, good-natured as always. Frank's "get to work" wife, as usual, had managed to skip over the pleasantries and dive straight into doling out the chores.

"I'm sorry," she said, facing her husband squarely and smiling sweetly. "Hi, Honey." She touched his cheek briefly before putting her purse down into his just vacated kitchen chair and adding, "And by the way Frank, there's a nice big heavy sack of kibble in the truck for Candy, too!" Trudy reached down to pat the yellow dog's head, noticing for the millionth time the almost non-existent torn ear and wincing slightly. Candy was a medium sized mixed breed dog and a central figure of the family. Always loved as the family pet, she became cherished as their hero after fighting off a supposedly mythological, but sadly all too real, chupacabra. Trudy spoke to the dog. "Yes, Candy, Mama got you some nice kibble and a couple of dried pig ears for an extra special treat!" She looked around to make sure the family was out unloading the truck. She didn't want them to catch her talking to Candy like Frank's mother spoke to that chihuahua of hers.

Turning her attention to the shopping bags, Trudy began to unload the cans of black beans and tuna fish from the first green sack. She glanced at the maps beneath the bags, only mildly curious as to what her family was up to, and saw various topographical maps, with widely spread contour lines indicating areas of flatter, lower elevations. "Certainly not around here," she thought. She leant in to take a closer look, and frowned, somewhat puzzled. "Laos, Thailand, the Philippines, Cambodia? What *are* they up to?" Shifting a can of crushed tomatoes, Trudy became even more curious. "And Texas?"

***

Philo sat at his desk, virtually building a Lego model of a Tyrannosaurus Rex on his computer. He had long ago stopped fiddling directly with the colorful little plastic bricks. Whenever he wanted to change something about a model he was working on, having to dismantle the whole thing became just too tedious. So Philo, at age thirteen, devised a way to do the initial planning on his desktop. He could assemble the thing in three dimensions on the screen, and then print out instructions for real-world building as though he had purchased a kit. Of course, after he came up with the program, he discovered software already in existence that could do the same thing, but for Philo, the best thing about being smart was being independent; being able to figure stuff out on your own without having to wait for a grown-up to help you out or drive you to the mall. Since his mom and dad had started up their new business last summer, he hadn't been seeing a lot of them anyway.

Philo glanced down at the real gold brick keeping his bedroom door ajar. He and his cousins had had a wonderful adventure last summer and the gold brick had been a surprisingly insignificant part of the reward. The excitement and fun of discovering the Ruminators (a group of mutant talking goats of all things!), and getting to know his cousins Shawn and Marsha had been the real payoff. Still, the brick was worth a ton of money and Philo had tried giving it to his parents, hoping to help ease them through the hardship of starting their new business in the current tough economy. Dad naturally refused, saying, "No dice, Son! Imagine how much a decent University education will cost!" And Mom had added, "...through to your doctorate degree!" much to Philo's chagrin. "Heck, I'm sure to get at least a couple of scholarships!" he had argued to their predictably stony silence. So the gold brick sat on the floor and he sat in an empty apartment.

The phone rang, the land line down the hall, startling Philo and he jumped slightly before swiveling his chair and getting up to answer it. His bare feet made little sound in the quiet apartment and the phone's ringing seemed deafening. The voice on the other end was loud too; familiar, cheerful, and with excellent timing.

"Hey, Cuz," Philo replied into the receiver, "I was just looking at my nifty doorstop and thinking about our great adventure last summer!"

"Well, whaddya say," said Shawn drawing out his words, "ya wanna go on another one?"

2 The Next Adventure

Philo smiled knowingly. "Hmm, now wait a minute," he said. "Before I agree, will there be any mutant, snarling, blood sucking creatures in this new adventure?"

"Aww, sorry mate, no such luck this time," said Shawn, almost wishing there were. Last summer's adventure certainly was exciting; chasing down those chupacabras, or rather being chased *by* them! But maybe something a bit less perilous could be fun too? "Nope, no blood sucking mutants, just the opposite really. Dad's got info on some sightings of a really cute and fuzzy little critter that's supposed to be extinct. He wants us all to go check it out. And I don't mean Ivory-Billed Woodpecker extinct; I mean *really* extinct. Like forty million years extinct."

"You mean we're going looking for a Lingerling? Wow! Cool!" said Philo excitedly into the phone.

"No, not that. It's an Onomomo…mo…something. Heck, I forget what the thing's called, but it's not a Lingerling, whatever *that* is."

Philo smiled warmly into the empty apartment. Talking to Shawn was always entertaining. Philo's cousin was a bright guy, but one of the brightest things about him was that he would never pretend to understand something that he didn't; he was always open to learning something new. "Sorry to cause confusion, Shawn! A Lingerling isn't a specific animal. It's what you call a supposedly long extinct creature that's still around. Ya know *lingering* around? Like that woodpecker you mentioned. Or like the coelacanth. Remember? That weird lookin' fish that was thought to be extinct for like sixty-five million years until some guy actually caught one off the coast of Africa? Some folks think that the Loch Ness Monster might be a Lingerling. I've heard theories that ol' Nessie is a plesiosaur that somehow got lost on the way to extinction."

Down south in New Mexico, sitting at that still map covered Formica kitchen table, a puzzled look came over Shawn's face and he scratched his dark brown hair and looked into the receiver just as his sister came into the room for a glass of water. "Shawn, you must be talking to Philo," said Marsha. "You've got that 'What the heck is this guy talking about' look on your face."

Shawn put the receiver out toward his sister. "Here, you talk to him. I'm telling him about the camping trip Dad's got planned

9

for us all to go to Texas, and he's talking about see-low-somethings and the Loch Ness Monster." Shawn paused to cover the receiver with his other hand. "What a weird-o..."

Marsha grinned at her younger brother. Shawn was no dumb bunny, but Marsha felt he was put on this planet strictly for fun. Just an upbeat young guy who wasn't particularly interested in any of the details of their camping trip other than making sure they brought the sleeping bags and s'mores fixings. Shawn was not one to waste too much brain power thinking about the creature that their Dad was supposed to be looking for. That was the kind of guy cousin Philo was.

Marsha took the phone from her brother and spoke into the receiver. "Hey, Philo, Marsha here. So Shawn told you Mom and Dad have talked to your folks? No? Well, yeah, he'd forget small stuff like that, but don't worry; he'd never forget the marshmallows! Yep, it's all arranged. Your plane leaves Chicago on Tuesday and after a day or two lounging around Bernardo we'll be driving out to Texas to look for this living fossil."

"Awesome! I'm totally itching to get out of this apartment and back to New Mexico. Um, but Texas, you said?" Philo knitted his brow. "What's the story with this creature? Shawn seemed a tiny bit unclear..."

***

Hefting the same old duffle bag up the same old mobile home steps and through the Mater family's front door, Philo had a huge grin on his lightly freckled face. He was as excited and talkative as he was the first time he visited, just last summer, and possibly even more so owing to the adventure they all experienced during that unbelievable trip. He plopped his bag down on the floor, ran his hand through his sandy blonde hair and said, "So, Uncle Frank. This possible Lingerling. An omomyid, right? How many sightings have there been? Why do you think it could be the same creature that was around during the Eocene epoch? Was the person who saw it a reliable source? Have you spoken personally to him? What happens when we find it? I mean do we just photograph it, or capture it, or what? Hey, when do we get started?"

Frank stood up from the sofa where he had been looking at some maps of Texas. Regular road maps this time, planning the long drive to the eastern part of that state. He patted his nephew on the back and spoke merrily, "Hey Philo! Good to see you! Welcome back! You are just like your Aunt Trudy. No adherence to the usual social pleasantries! No 'hello, how are you, Uncle Frank?' You just jump into the meat of the conversation!"

"Well, ya know," interrupted Trudy, "it's a sign of a brain in motion! And Philo's brain is always in high gear. Your nephew had so many questions on the ride down from the airport, and Shawn and Marsha and I just weren't able to answer all of them. I almost pulled over to call you from the highway because we

11

weren't sure he could make it through the trip!" Trudy laughed, shutting the door behind her and the kids.

Frank pushed Candy off the sofa and gestured to Philo to sit down. "There you go Philo, Candy has preheated a nice warm spot for you on the couch. Sit and I'll tell you what I know." Philo reached down to pet Candy, whose tail was wagging round and round like a little helicopter rotor as he sat down next to his uncle. From the kitchen, Shawn asked if anyone wanted a soda and came back in the room with two cans in one hand and his other arm elbow deep in a bag of nacho cheese tortilla chips. He passed a soda to Philo and plopped down on the hassock, asking between crunches if the creature they were looking for might just possibly be carnivorous.

Marsha rolled her eyes and said, "Go on Dad, start at the beginning and maybe Shawn will listen this time." She gestured for her brother to fork over the bag of chips, took a small handful and passed the bag over to Philo.

"Okay," said Frank. "Here's what I know. It starts out a little like a bad joke." Frank paused to smile broadly at the group. "This guy goes into the Natural History Museum…"

"Stop me if you've heard this one," Shawn interrupted, laughing and licking nacho cheese dust from his finger tips.

"Yeah, well it was a new one on me," said Frank. "I heard it from a guy over at the Houston Zoo. We've been working out the details of transferring a new female lion from there.

Anyway, it seems he heard about this guy who saw a display of an omomyid at the Museum of Natural Science and he tells the guard that he saw a creature just like that when he was out hunting. The guard laughs and says that's ridiculous, but the guy insists he saw one, cute as a bug, he says, sitting in a tree and staring at him with its big eyes."

"Big eyes, Uncle Frank? What is this thing supposed to look like?"

"It's sort of like a tarsier," Frank replied, "A pretty close relative apparently." When Philo looked back at him with an uncharacteristic look of incomprehension on his usually intelligent face, Frank continued. "Tarsiers are a kind of small primate, real cute little guys, soft and furry and about the size of a squirrel, with big eyes and really long fingers and toes. That's where their name comes from. The tarsus bones in their feet are extra long and their toes have nails, like people, rather than claws. Today tarsiers are found living primarily in the islands of Southeast Asia. Here, there's a picture in this book." Frank passed the book to his nephew. "I'm surprised at you Philo, that you haven't done your research!" Marsha and Shawn leaned in towards Philo to get a closer look and Marsha let out an "aaaw" because of the creature's undeniable cuteness.

Philo laughed good-naturedly. "Well, I've been busy getting ready for this trip! You guys kind of sprung it on me pretty quickly and I decided I'd do better to research about Texas. I mean, I figured my zoologist uncle would have all the four-one-

one we'd need about the Lingerling!" Frank nodded in appreciation of his nephew's reasoning while Philo paused, considering the photo of the tarsier. "Yep, that's cute alright. So isn't it possible that if these things are so cute that what this guy saw was an escaped pet? You know, somebody goes on holiday to Thailand and brings one back illegally but it bites him on the finger or poops on the Persian rug and they chuck it out into the woods," posed Philo.

"True, that kind of thing happens a lot. People irresponsibly releasing unwanted exotic pets or even plant material into the wild. But it's not so likely with tarsiers. Cute though they may be, tarsiers are not pet material. Not at all. For one thing, they are nearly impossible to keep in captivity. Touching a tarsier, no matter what the intention, is almost certain to result in the creature's death. We, and by that I mean zoologists, aren't exactly sure why, perhaps it's disease transmission, or maybe humans are just not good at taking care of their nutritional needs, but tarsiers in captivity generally die." Frank, animal lover that he was, allowed a look of sadness to flicker quickly across his face before adding merrily, "And by the way, Shawn, for your information, tarsiers *are* carnivorous! In fact they're the only *totally* carnivorous primates! But not to worry, they mostly eat insects. They couldn't eat anything remotely as big as a Shawn!" Frank laughed loudly, looking around at his family, who apparently weren't as amused with his joke as he had been. "Hmm," he said, shifting on the sofa and crossing his arms as though gathering his thoughts up into them, "I digress.

The creature that the guy said he saw staring at him from the branches of a tree in East Texas, at least according to what he said, more closely resembled the long extinct Eocene era omomyid that used to live in the area because it had smaller eyes and it was looking at him in broad daylight. It wasn't, apparently, nocturnal."

"So we're going looking for this thing, this tiny critter, just based on one guy's story?" asked Shawn. "Sounds like looking for a squirrel in a haystack."

"At least we'll have one nut to use as bait," said Marsha, pointing from behind her hand at her brother.

"Good one, Sis!" said Shawn with honest appreciation.

3 Setting Out

Philo spent the next two days hanging around with his cousins, enjoying trips into town in Marsha's little yellow truck for pizza and other snacks, and researching what he could over the internet about tarsiers and omomyids. He wanted to remember every detail about the creatures, their differences and similarities, hoping to find an authentic Lingerling. Although he was very excited about the prospect, it was unusually difficult for him to concentrate being so near to Ladron Peak, the big mountain whose foothills were just a stone's throw from the Mater family's house. Only last summer they had battled and won against General Schwinger's mutant chupacabras to rescue the gentle Ruminators. Philo hadn't of course seen any of the sentient goat-like creatures with the human hands and feet since his return home to Chicago, and he was curious to find out how they were. Apparently the herd was intact, living in secret down in southern New Mexico. Frank said it would be possible to drive down there and catch up with Gadget and Salizar and the rest of the herd when they returned from the Texas trip. Philo sure hoped so. He had even brought along in his duffle bag some old oddities like a transistor radio and an 8-track tape of Elvis Presley; human artifacts that he wanted to give to Basher, a young buck who had a fondness for such things. In the meantime, Philo wanted to figure out for himself what the story was with this possible Lingerling. Of course, Frank knew quite a bit about the living creature, the tarsier, what there was to know at least, but this other creature, the one sighted in an eastern Texas forest... Could it really be an omomyid? And if so, how it could still be living in Texas without being seen for forty million years?

***

At last the morning came when the three teens and the zoologist were ready to set out in Trudy's truck. Trudy and Candy had both declined to come on the trip; Trudy because she had some design work she needed to get done for a fledgling space tourism company that was starting up at the new SpacePort down south, and Candy because she would just love to find, and unfortunately eat, every squirrel-sized mammal in Texas. It was still dark when Marsha held the gate open for her dad as he drove the pickup out through the barbed wire fence surrounding the property. Although the Maters only owned five acres, there wasn't another neighbor for at least half a mile, with the next house being another half a mile beyond them. It gave the Maters a feeling of being land barons, even of this

17

scruffy desert where they had lived since before the kids were born. As Marsha hopped back into the truck, taking her place in the front passenger seat, Philo looked out the window from his seat in the king cab behind his Uncle. He could see the twinkling lights of the interstate off in the distance and the lights from two or three distant mobile homes. There weren't many "real" houses out here in Bernardo, the kind that sat on permanent foundations, and Philo liked the feeling of travel and movement that he got from this place. The mobile homes, the freeway exit with its billboards, the old abandoned gas station, the RV Park. He also liked the feeling of getting up early with the nighttime desert chill still in the air and driving off into the dark without any street lights to show the way. Suddenly, a coyote crossed the dirt road, just at the far reaches of Frank's high beams. It wasn't in any hurry, this was his time and his place and the coyote looked at the truck as though it were a temporary interloper that would soon be moving out. Philo pointed and grinned. "Hey, Shawn, didja see that? Shawn?"

Shawn lifted his head from its drooped position on his chest. "Wha? Are we there yet?" he mumbled. "Hey Marsha, pass me a pop-tart wouldya?"

"Aw Shawn, ya missed the coyote!" said Philo, sad that his cousin missed seeing the animal.

"It's okay, Philo," said Shawn with a dozy voice. "The main thing is that Dad missed it… With the truck, I mean."

18

***

The truck hummed along Route 60 with Frank at the wheel, and the other occupants passed the time listening to the radio, reading, or just looking out the window watching the New Mexico landscape go by. With the sun long up and a few hundred miles having passed by under the wheels of the pickup, Frank pulled off the highway for a rest and some lunch. As they passed the usual roadside gas station and truck stop diner and headed south, Shawn looked up from the graphic novel he was reading and swiveled his face toward the empty road ahead. A worried expression came across his usually sunny face as he pointed his thumb towards the truck bed and said, "Hey Dad, the restaurant's back there," with some slight note of panic in his voice.

"It's okay Shawn, your mom packed a cooler," said Frank. "With all your favorites," he added, achieving the calming effect he had intended. "I thought we'd have a picnic and do a bit of sight-seeing along the way!" Frank checked his rear view mirror looking for signs of comprehension on the faces of his passengers. "Kids, you all realize this isn't a serious expedition don't you? I mean, we're not expecting to actually find this living fossil; it's just a good excuse to get out and see the world! You know, a vacation for your old dad. The Albuquerque Biopark isn't funding this trip. If they were, you guys would not be my first choice for a serious research team," said Frank, adding, "...no offence," as he glanced at his nephew over his shoulder.

"None taken, Uncle Frank!" said Philo with a grin. "Maybe we *won't* be making any earth shattering discoveries on this trip, but someday I may well be more than just a kid with a smartphone! You might be calling on me to *lead* an expedition!"

"I have no doubt, my genius nephew!" said Frank in all seriousness, gesturing with his chin towards a sign off to the left. "Ahh, here we are. Get ready to disembark!"

"Aaw Dad, what's this place? I was hoping we were gonna take a detour to Roswell. I really could use some new alien action figures for my collection! Plus, I lost one of the greys from my chess set!" said Shawn. Ever since he was small, Shawn had a fascination for aliens and the family had made several pilgrimages to Roswell to visit the crash site, the museum, the McDonald's shaped like a UFO, and, most importantly, the gift shops. Interspersed with the Lego bricks that coated Shawn's bedroom floor were many plastic representations of aliens in styles ranging from the cuddly to the grotesque. Each one had been carefully collected and coveted over the years. Shawn could spend hours in one of the tacky gift shops, weighing the attributes of one alien over another in an effort to get as much bang for his souvenir buck as was humanly possible. Shawn's favorite figure was a little smiling red alien figure whose body parts, for some strange and probably otherworldly reason, folded up inside of its hollow head.

Marsha looked up from the novel she was reading. "Where we are, Dad? Doesn't look like Roswell. Not an alien in sight." She hadn't said a word for miles, being totally engrossed in her book.

"Nope, no aliens. Roswell is quite a bit further south. We're near Clovis… Portales, actually. Pretty close to the Texas border. Maybe we can swing by Roswell on the way back, but today I wanted to take you to see Blackwater Draw. You probably don't remember, Marsha, but I took you and Shawn out here years ago. I thought Philo might be interested to see this place too. That's why we've headed out on Route 60 rather than take the quick way through Albuquerque on the Interstate."

"Oh, have we been on sixty all this time? I totally missed Mountainair! I guess I really haven't been paying attention. I sure could use a pit stop to stretch my limbs. And a clean restroom would be awesome!" declared Marsha.

"That must be some good book you're reading, Marsha. All you did was grunt at us when we stopped about an hour ago at that gas station," said Philo, craning his neck in between the front seats in an attempt to see the dust jacket.

"Yeah," interrupted Shawn. "I couldn't believe it when you waved away the doughnuts! A book that's better than a chocolate glazed? You'll have to let me borrow it when you're finished, Sis."

21

"Sure thing, little bro. You'll like this one; it's about your favorite grey aliens who invade a small desert town! I'm just to the part where all kinds of crazy stuff starts to happen!" Marsha made an eerie theremin-like noise as she pushed a paper napkin into the book to mark her place. Frank smiled at his daughter as he swung the truck into the nearly empty dirt lot and chose a spot next to a juniper tree hoping for a little shade to park in. The four of them got out of the truck, all stretching their limbs and looking around.

"So what's to see here, Dad?" asked Shawn.

"Well, we'll check out the museum first and then we'll have some lunch out at the actual site. Certainly you guys are familiar with the Clovis culture, right? They're the people considered to be the first human inhabitants of our so-called New World. Well, this spot near here is where some artifacts were found back in the 1930's that gave those people the name Clovis."

"I vaguely remember this place," said Marsha. "I remember the arrow heads."

Frank opened the door to the building and a nice cool air met them. "Yes, that's right Marsha. The first artifacts they found, and the most distinctive, were spear points made from stone. Some of the points have been found in sites that also contain mammoth remains and the remains of other extinct creatures like giant sloths."

Shawn rolled his eyes in mock surprise. "So people have *always* been trying to kill and eat every animal on the planet? It isn't just me and my love of bacon?"

Marsha posed a question to her Dad. "Do you think that humans caused them to be wiped out? I've heard that people hunted those animals to extinction."

"Well, I'm not sure about that. I have a feeling climate played a part. I mean, look at this landscape now. It's hard to imagine that creatures as big as elephants could ever find enough to eat out here. Why don't we go and look at the exhibits and see what we can find out."

"You boys get started and I'll catch you up," said Marsha. "What I most urgently need to find out is the way to the Ladies' Room!"

4 Crossing the Border

"Say farewell to Texico, hello to Farwell!" sang out Frank with an exaggerated twang to his voice as they crossed the border from New Mexico into Texas. "We'll be resting our heads under the Texas stars tonight!" Frank smiled. He was pleased to be out on the open road. Although he loved his job at the Albuquerque Biopark, and loved their Bernardo home as well, Frank was happiest when he was out on a ramble. Especially so if backpacking and sleeping out under the stars were included.

"Ooh Dad, stop so I can take a picture for Mom. We can stand our mess right next to the 'Don't Mess with Texas' sign!" said Marsha fishing the little digital camera out of the leather bag at her feet.

In the seat behind her, Shawn crossed his arms. "Hey, I'm not such a mess!" he said, putting on a cartoonishly grumpy face.

Philo and Frank both giggled appreciatively as Marsha asked sweetly, "Gee, Shawn, what in the world made you think I was talking about you?"

***

Trudy and Candy were comfortably positioned in the living room back in Bernardo, each on her own sofa, feet and paws up respectively, spending their first evening alone just relaxing. Trudy had a policy not to allow the dog up on the furniture. When Frank and the kids were home, Trudy usually made a show of shoving the yellow dog down to her own dog bed on the floor, but when it was just the two of them, the old girls, Trudy called them in her mind, Candy got spoiled and pampered. The dog certainly deserved a soft place to lay down after her heroic battle with the chupacabra, but for Trudy, it was more than that. The whole strange adventure of last summer had put her family back together, both physically and in less tangible ways, and Candy had played a brave part.

The mystery of Frank's sudden and unexplained disappearance had been solved. Frank had come back from his strange imprisonment bringing danger with him, but the frightening events that followed had made Trudy's family tighter. Even the previously embattled siblings Marsha and Shawn had gained a new respect for one another, and a close friendship had developed with their cousin Philo. Of course Candy, now six years the family's pet, wasn't responsible for all of that, but Trudy needed someone to lavish her continued warm and grateful feelings on. Trudy's stoic New Mexico ranch upbringing would not allow her to spoil her kids or husband, no matter how much she would really like to, but spoiling a dog, at least when no one was looking, was another thing entirely. Candy complied happily; an eager and willing recipient of the love that Trudy doled out in private.

The television was on, but the program was terrible; just meandering noise filling the room in an effort to keep Trudy company. The quiet of the house was unsettlingly unusual, but Trudy switched the set off anyway and went into the kitchen, planning to enjoy a cup of peppermint tea before turning in for the night. Tomorrow's list of to-dos was all ready and waiting for morning on the kitchen table. Number one on the list was to clean the house and catch up on the laundry so that her physical and mental space would be clear before tackling the ad campaign for Terra Taurus Space Tours. "How and why did I agree to get myself involved with an outer space tourism company?" she wondered aloud, trying not to think about it until tomorrow. Candy picked her head up off of her paws and looked at Trudy, ready to get off the sofa at the confusing human's whim. "Okay Candy, whaddya say you and I go outside and look at the stars over Ladron Peak?"

Fragrantly steaming mug in hand, Trudy opened the door for Candy, and watched as the dog ever so slowly put her front paws down onto the floor and arched her back in a lazy stretch. Candy took her time following up with her back feet before she was completely off the sofa and making her approach to the door. "Jeez, dog, you've let in just about all the moths in New Mexico and a few from Arizona too, I don't doubt!" Trudy grimaced and then admitted aloud, "Okay, I was the one holding the door open, but c'mon Candy, let's move it." Oblivious to the criticism, Candy trotted happily down the steps, her one ear flapping. Trudy followed slowly, letting her eyes become accustomed to the dark.

The moon hadn't risen yet and the Mater family didn't believe in turning on any outside lights unless they absolutely had to. Most of the people who lived in the area preferred for their yards to stay dark at night, but occasionally a newbie would move in, plunk down a mobile home and install some mega-bright light onto their power pole. Usually the light would get turned off permanently after a few weeks when the inhabitants realized that the desert was supposed to be dark at night. Lighting the night always seemed to make it appear to be much darker out there anyway. At the edges of the pools of light, the transition to the unlit areas were like stepping suddenly off a cliff to where the night was black, deep and absolute. Sure, you could go out into your yard and mosey around in the small circle of light, but the circle would almost feel as though it had walls around it, black walls of nothing.

One of the best things about living in Bernardo was the sky. For Trudy, bright blue days and star filled nights were a major advantage of country living. Some folks might see the place as barren desert, but without much in the way of trees or buildings to impede the view, the sky was an incredible source of beauty.

Having a bright light outside would only have the effect of obliterating the night sky, the moonlit mesas, and the dramatically looming Ladron Peak. Trudy and Frank had long ago realized that if you couldn't see the stars, then what was the purpose of living in a planetarium? They felt bad for the folks who lived in Albuquerque, whose bright lights could be seen as a small curved area of glow on the horizon. Sure, city dwellers could get in their cars and drive to the darkness, but one of the best delights of a cool evening in Bernardo was to haul out the telescope and marvel at the visible universe from the comfort of your own yard.

Another drawback of lighting the night, and something Trudy particularly disliked, was that turning on the outside lights brought bugs. Night bugs that stayed hidden during the heat of the day would normally come out to cluster on the windows, some of them truly giant moths and groups of praying mantises, and sitting on a lit porch would have them hovering around your head, crawling down your neck, and diving into any open beverage. Although the presence of the bugs at dusk would be a call to the acrobatic bats to swoop and hunt, mostly the night insects would just squeeze into the house and bang endlessly and annoyingly against the table lamps.

Trudy adjusted the cushions on the sofa-sized swing and settled down into them. She smiled as she inhaled the aroma of the peppermint tea and gazed out at the night sky. The shape of Ladron Peak was visible to the west. Although the night was dark, the mountain was darker and no lights could be seen in that direction other than stars. The night was deliciously cool after the heat of the day and soon Trudy had finished her tea, set the mug down on the sandy ground and was drifting off to sleep with Candy curled up at her feet.

***

Frank sat in the driver's seat and peered at a crumpled map of Texas spread across his lap. Marsha had gotten her photo of the group standing in front of the sign marking the border from New Mexico into Texas, unspectacular though it was, and they needed to plan where they would spend the night. "Alright guys, what's it gonna be? Bedtime in Muleshoe or Bovine?" he asked.

"Are there any National Forests or State Parks nearby, Uncle Frank? I sure would love a night under the stars," said Philo, hoping that his uncle wasn't intending for them to find a motel room.

"Hmm, let's see," said Frank, scanning the map for telltale green areas with little tent-shaped icons. "Well, looks like Muleshoe it is then! But it will probably be pretty dark when we get there. We'll have to set up camp by headlights."

"That's okay, Dad," said Marsha. "We don't need to pitch the tent. It's beautiful weather for just lying out in a sleeping bag under the stars!"

"You know I won't put up a fight!" agreed Frank, who was always happiest out of doors. "Let's see if we can buy us a bucket of fried chicken and head for the campsite!"

"What do ya say to two buckets, Dad?" asked Shawn rubbing his midsection. "And a coupla sides and maybe some biscuits to go with?"

5 Under the Stars

Trudy blearily opened her eyes and looked around her. For a moment she was confused. It was dark, it was chilly, just where was she? Then she remembered. The tea, the swing, the beautiful night sky full of stars. She sat up and stretched. "Looks like us old girls fell asleep, eh Candy?" Trudy reached down to retrieve the empty mug, meaning to bring it back to the house where she would put it in the sink with the rest of the day's dishes to be done in the morning. Then she would get herself ready for bed properly by brushing her teeth and putting on her favorite nightshirt. The delicious thought of an entire bed to sprawl about in suddenly made Trudy feel lonely. Just like how she felt night after night last year when Frank's whereabouts were unknown. But she knew exactly where her husband was tonight, so a night alone in a bed should be seen as a treat. Perhaps she would let Candy sleep on top of the bedspread. Just this once…

Trudy's hand searched blindly underneath the swing for the mug. Finally she felt the cool of the ceramic handle and grasped it, lifting it up off of the ground only to instantly drop it as the night sky was suddenly lit up by an intensely bright flash. A streak of fire shot out like a rocket from beyond Ladron Peak and flew high over Trudy's head, disappearing in the east. The light only lasted a moment and there was no sound associated with it, no sonic boom or jet engine noise, only the sound of splintering glass as the mug Trudy was holding slipped from her grasp, smashed down onto a stone, and shattered into pieces. "Yowza, Candy, what the heck was that? Did you see that thing? Wow, I've seen some meteor showers before, but that thing was either very big, or very close! Spectacular!" She craned her neck upwards, both hoping for and fearing a reoccurrence. Trudy wondered out loud "What could that have been?" before realizing with a start what had become of the ceramic cup. "Oh jeez, Frank's gonna kill me. That was his favorite mug!"

***

Snug in his sleeping bag, Shawn awoke to someone or some *thing* poking him frantically in the ribs. "Whaa..? Issit Bigfoot?" was all he managed to mutter before hearing his cousin Philo whispering in his ear.

"Shawn! You awake?" he hissed. "Didja see that? Wow that was amazing! A huge meteor just flew over! Didja see?"

Nonplussed and more than half asleep, Shawn replied, "Yikes, calm down, Cuz. I told ya not to wake me unless you see Bigfoot! Go back to sleep!" The sleepy teen turned over and scrunched down lower into his sleeping bag. His voice came drowsily up out of the bag, muffled by the down filling. "Tell me all about it tomorrow."

"But Shawn," protested his excited cousin, "it was amazing! A huge, I mean, really huge, and um, and bright, like a gigantic fireball! Wow! I'm, I'm, I'm…"

"Speechless, are you?" grumbled Shawn. "Good. Then shut up and go to sleep!"

Philo finally did as he was told, or at least he tried to. The flash of light that had cut through the darkness overhead was like no shooting star that the city-dweller had ever seen. "If that was a meteorite," Philo thought, "it must have fallen somewhere east of here. I sure would like to find it!" He lay on his back for some thirty minutes or more, trying to keep his eyes closed, but they kept popping open to gaze at the stars between the treetops in hopes of seeing a repeat performance. Eventually, sleep overcame and he drifted off, dreaming of finding a huge glowing asteroid or a red ball of steaming space junk, like something from an old episode of Lost in Space.

***

The next morning found all the campers, including Shawn, up early with the rising sun. The unimproved campsite they were at was empty of any other campers, being more of a local weekend spot. Shawn squinted and blinked, rubbing his eyes with one hand as he attempted to shove his sleeping bag into its sack with the other. "Jeez, I knew there was a reason I liked sleeping in a tent! This 'under the stars' thing let's that big bright star shine right in my eyes!"

"That big bright star?" said Frank with a laugh. "You mean the sun, right? Well, it's good we're up early. For one thing we'll be getting back on the road sooner. I'd like to make it out to where that alleged omomyid was spotted by nightfall. I think it'll be a snap if we don't make too many stops."

"Hey, Uncle Frank, did you happen to see that other big bright star last night?" asked Philo. "I don't know if it was a meteorite or what, but it flew right over and was really huge and really bright. I know we don't get to see much in the way of stars in Chicago, I mean, I haven't got a lot to compare it to, but this had to have been out of the ordinary."

"Nope Philo, guess I missed it. I was asleep as soon as my head hit the ground. And boy, was it hard!" said Frank, rubbing his lower back. "I swear the ground is harder here in Texas than it is in New Mexico."

"Oh, Dad," said Marsha, laughing, "the ground hasn't gotten harder; it's your back that's gotten softer!"

Frank frowned at his eldest child. "I'll have you know I am in fine shape for a man my age. I don't know who you've been talking to!" Just as Frank crossed his arms to punctuate his displeasure at being called soft, the phone in Frank's pocket started to buzz. He took it out and looked at the screen. "Okay, nobody tell your mom about my sore back!" Frank pressed a button and spoke into the receiver. "Oh hey, honey, we were just talking about you!"

"With fondness, I hope?" replied Trudy with a cheerful tone to her voice.

"Sure thing! I was just saying how your daughter sometimes sounds exactly like you!" said Frank, giving Marsha a wink.

"Hmm," said Trudy thoughtfully, "I'm not so sure that sounds too nice at all!" She changed to a more pouting tone and continued. "And here I was missing you! I just woke up next to Candy instead of you and I wanted to say good morning to someone with better breath! I'm sorry if I'm calling too early..."

"I'm not so sure I qualify about the better breath," said Frank moving his tongue over his teeth. "I fell deep asleep as soon as my head hit the pillow last night, without brushing. But I guess the phone will act as a sort of long distance mouthwash!"

"Hmm," said Trudy again, wanting to change the subject from morning breath. "Say, I was sitting outside on the swing last night, enjoying the stars and the cool night air when I saw the most amazing shooting star. Actually, I'm not sure that's what it was. A meteor, I guess. Or is it a meteorite? Stalactite, stalagmite, let's call the whole thing off," Trudy joked.

"Anyway, it was amazing. I'm afraid I broke your snake mug. It was so huge and bright. The meteor, I mean. It startled me and I dropped your mug and broke it. Sorry."

"It's alright. I'm sure the Rattlesnake Museum gift shop will have another," said Frank. "Ya know, Philo was just telling us about a meteor that he saw last night. I guess it's possible that you could've seen the same one; we're not *that* far away. Although, it would have to have been a pretty big object for you both to see it."

"Or whatever it was it could have been entering the atmosphere at too steep or shallow an angle, Unk," said Philo. "If an object enters the atmosphere at what would be a wrong angle, too much friction would cause it to totally burn up in a huge fireball!" It was obvious that the boy from Chicago was enjoying himself immensely.

"Hey, didja hear that Trude? Maybe that's some info you could use for the Terra Taurus campaign. Make sure in any sketches you do that you draw the re-entry angle right, or -poof- there goes the space tourist trade!"

"I'll keep that in mind!" said Trudy, actually making a mental note to Google it. "So speaking of the tourist trade, what are your plans for today? Where are you guys anyway?"

"We spent the night sleeping under the stars in Muleshoe, Texas. You know what the song says." Frank paused to clear his throat before singing, "…the stars at night, are big and bright…"

Marsha and Shawn clapped on cue and joined in with the remainder: "...deep in the heart of Texas!" loud enough for Trudy to hear over the phone and she smiled. "Well, except that you're just barely over the border! Same stars here as there. Philo and I are testament to that," she added.

Frank laughed appreciatively. "Plans for today? Hmm, well we hadn't discussed it, but I know Shawn wanted to show Philo the Cadillac Ranch, and I want to get where we're going. Seeing as how I'm doing the driving, I think we'll make a beeline for the forest and start looking for that omomyid in the morning or maybe I should go by the museum and find out if we could talk to that hunter who saw it in the first place. Hmm, we might not be able to make it there during the museums open hours, so..." Frank paused in thought. "Gee, I guess I should've planned a bit better. Anyway, we should get a move on. Alright Trudy, you get some work done on your outer space stuff, and we'll talk to you later...Yeah, we'll call and let you know where we get to and what we get up to. Love ya. Bye." Frank pressed the "end" button as the kids yelled "Bye, Mom!" in the back ground.

"So no Cadillac Ranch today, Dad?" asked Shawn, with the disappointment changing his usually smiling expression.

"Cadillac Ranch? What's that?" asked Philo. "Sounds like the name of a Texas-style used car dealership!"

"Oh Philo, not at all. You'd like it. It's art, I guess ya call it, but it's really just a bunch of old cars stuck in the ground. Cadillacs. Kind of like a post-apocalyptic Stonehenge!" explained Shawn.

"Sounds cool," said Philo, enthusiastic as always. "How about it, Uncle Frank?"

"Well, I was thinking we'd head off and start looking for the omomyid, but I'd really want to talk to the hunter who saw it first. I dunno why I didn't try and call the guy before we left home... Tell ya what, let's see if I can get the info over the phone and that would loosen up our time schedule some. You know, it may be summer break for you kids, but my vacation time is limited; the animals always need you when you're a zoologist. I am *totally* into seeing all the sights in Texas, but I *do* have to get back to work at some point!"

6 Deep in the Heart

Once again in their same seats in the pickup truck with their camping gear safely stowed in the back, Frank was driving east and apologizing to his son. "For some reason, I was thinking that The Cadillac Ranch was down off I-10. Sorry, Shawn, we'll make sure we go by Amarillo on the way home. That way we can stop in Albuquerque at the Rattlesnake Museum and get me a new snake mug," said Frank with a chuckle. "But tell ya what, I've spoken to the guy who saw our alleged Lingerling and he told me where he saw it, GPS coordinates and everything, and where the best spots are for camping nearby. He says he was out shooting dove when he saw it, but the season's over now, so happily we won't have to worry about getting shot!"

"Well, that sure is a plus for me, Dad!" said Marsha, only half-joking.

Shawn was still hoping to swing by the Roswell gift shops on their return trip, so he was considering voicing his displeasure about taking the northern route home when his father spoke again. "Now I figure we'll have time for a little bit of sight-seeing before we get to the forest, so what'll it be?" Frank asked. "The World's Largest Doughnuts, or the Inner Space Caverns?"

"Gee, Dad!" exclaimed Shawn brightly. "Do you really have to ask? Giant doughnuts of course!" Shawn instantly replaced his thoughts of plastic alien figures with thoughts of deep-fried sugary goodness. "Dooough-nuts!"

"I for one vote for the caverns," said Marsha, politely raising her hand. "What do you say, Philo? Want to break the tie?"

Philo shook his head. "You sure know how to put a guy on the spot, dontcha? Sure, I'd like to break the tie, but I still want you *and* Shawn to be glad you brought me along! Any chance we could do it all, Uncle Frank? I should think a giant doughnut would taste unbelievably great in a cold dark cave. It certainly would have been welcome when we were lost in those old mining tunnels under Ladron Peak!" said Philo.

"Jeez, you're right!" said Marsha with a shudder. "I swore I'd never want to go underground again, and here I am voting to visit a cavern just for the fun of it!" Marsha looked thoughtful. "I guess since we had a happy ending that last time we went below the surface… And I sure do like the sound of the place… Inner Space Caverns! Sounds other worldly! Hey, maybe there'll be a gift shop, Shawn," she said, trying to tempt her brother away from the doughnuts, "one that sells underground aliens!"

"Alrighty then!" said Frank decisively. "I'm thinking it sounds like a consensus has been reached! Doughnuts As Big As Your Head *and* Inner Space Caverns *and* then on to Davy Crockett National Forest! I'll show you who's soft! Look out attractions, here we come!"

***

The sun was going down; sunlight slanting through the trees causing a flickering effect in the cab of the pickup. Shawn groaned with every bump as they bounced up and down on the rough dirt forest service road. They were driving in the Davy Crockett National Forest looking for the parking area that marked the trailhead down which their supposed Lingerling had been spotted. Shawn looked glumly out the window at the trees. So many trees. All kinds of trees. Loblolly pine trees, various kinds of oak trees, willow trees, hickory trees. Trees as far as the eye could see, which wasn't very far on account of all the trees. Shawn groaned again.

From up in the front passenger seat Marsha called back, "Whassa matter Shawn? Tummy ache? That sure was some doughnut, hunh? I can't believe you ate that whole thing, and finished mine off, too!"

"Ooooh, you don't have to remind me!" said Shawn, his voice sounding weak and decidedly remorseful. He swallowed hard, his mouth desert dry. "Dad, any chance there's a nice smooth paved road ahead, with a motel that has a nice soft bed?" Shawn closed his eyes and leaned back. "I don't feel too well. Even a hammock strung between some of these trees would be nice…"

Philo tried hard not to chuckle. Of course it was Shawn's own fault if he was feeling poorly. No one told Shawn to gorge himself. But he did seem to be in some discomfort, and Philo wanted to be kind. Mostly. "It's a good thing that we *didn't* make an underground picnic of those giant doughnuts after all!" he said. "We'd still be trying to pry Shawn out of those caverns if he had made a pig of himself down there. Thanks for taking us, Uncle Frank! That sure was wonderful to see!"

"You are most welcome, Philo," said Frank, making a deep sighing noise. "I for one am getting rather tired. The trailhead parking lot should be pretty near here. We'll set up camp there and get a good night's sleep. I just hope the ground's softer than last night in Muleshoe…Looks like I might get a nice bed of pine needles…" Frank shifted in his seat, remembering how his back had felt that morning. "Kids, I'm not particularly bothered about dinner. I'm really not so hungry after all that…um…well… You guys can make a sandwich from the stuff in the cooler if you want. I just want to sleep." At the mere mention of a sandwich, Shawn let out another, somewhat more urgent sounding, groan. "Don't worry, Son, we'll walk off that doughnut tomorrow. The part of the forest that we're headed for is strictly foot traffic only, no trucks, so we'll be backpacking. You'll soon be free of that huge pastry!"

"Oh, oh, stop the truck, Dad! I think I'm gonna be free of it right now!" said Shawn in a rush of misery, jumping out as soon as Frank set the hand brake and losing his share of the biggest doughnuts in the world behind the nearest tree.

***

The next morning, everyone woke feeling energetic and ready to go on a long hike, even Shawn. They had stopped at a spot designated for tent camping where they would safely be able to leave Trudy's truck and go the rest of the trip on foot, taking their food, water, and shelter in the packs on their backs. It was just before eight in the morning when they were ready to set off, having finished all the milk in the cooler by pouring it on their bowls of granola. Just as they were hoisting their packs up onto their backs, a cloud of dust on the road announced the arrival of a park ranger. He pulled up next to the group astride a small brown four-wheeler and they exchanged pleasantries. "You all got your permit displayed on your dashboard?" said the man in the short-sleeved brown uniform shirt and jeans. "I come by every day or so, just to make sure nobody's lost out there."

"Oh jeez, I'm sorry, I totally forgot to get a back-country permit!" said Uncle Frank, putting his palm to his forehead.

"It's okay, I've got some with me. Just fill in your license number, today's date and when you figure on being back, so I'll know if y'all need rescuing," chuckled the man, adjusting his brown park ranger bill cap so that it rested higher on his forehead.

"Oh, we'll be okay, we know where we're going," said Shawn. "We've got a GPS device *and* we're backing it up with an old fashioned compass!"

"We're going looking for that omomyid," Frank told the ranger. When the man gave him a puzzled look, Frank explained, "A hunter said he saw a strange animal out here and we came to check it out. I'm Dr. Frank Mater, I'm with the Albuquerque zoo." He stuck out his hand for the man to shake.

The ranger took the offered hand and let out a horsey sounding guffaw. "Oh yeah, I heard about you comin' out. Are these your research assistants?" he laughed heartily but stopped mid-snort. "No offence."

"We're used to it," said Philo with a shrug.

The park ranger smiled and continued, "That guy who saw the thing? Chuck? Chuck Shepherd? He's always seein' stuff out there. I hope you guys aren't seriously expecting to find no missing link or anything. Heck, ol' Chuck says he saw Bigfoot out there once!" The man laughed again, good naturedly, as Shawn's eyes grew large at the mention of his favorite elusive cryptid.

"Oh, we're more on a vacation than an expedition. Looking for Mr. Shepherd's omomyid is really just an excuse to go camping somewhere new with the kids. We like having a goal, whether it's real or imaginary!" said Frank.

"C'mon, Uncle Frank," interrupted Philo, "don't forget, last summer these 'assistants' of yours went off in search of lost gold treasure and actually found it!"

The park ranger showed only mild surprise, being more interested in getting back on the ATV and driving through the forest than hanging around in a parking lot talking to some out of state tourists. "Alright, well, you folks have fun, and fill that permit out and leave it where I can see it on your dashboard. When you get back you come to the ranger station and tell us all about your discovery. Maybe bring ol' Bigfoot in fer a Coke or somethin'!"

The three teenagers watched as the ranger drove off, while Frank fumbled through Trudy's glove compartment in search of a pen. He lent on the hood of the pickup to fill out the form and then turned to the kids. "Alright, gang, Mr. Shepherd said to head due east from the trailhead. He said the path was pretty well marked for the first two and a half miles and then we head southeast following some cairns."

"Cairns, did you say, Uncle Frank?" asked Philo. "I've heard of lap dogs called cairn terriers, but I've never heard of them being used as trail guides!" he added, laughing.

"Gosh, Philo, even I know that cairns are little piles of rocks that mark a trail," said Shawn. "Although I imagine Toto used little piles of something else to mark the yellow brick road!" Shawn smiled and let out a loud "ha!" in appreciation of his own joke.

Marsha rolled her eyes. "Shawn, what are you on about?" she asked.

Frank smirked. "Your brother is making what might loosely be called a pun. Toto in the movie version of *The Wizard of Oz* was a cairn terrier," he added, filling in the blanks. "Sometimes, Shawn, maybe your jokes are a little obscure?"

"No, not obscure, obtuse!" giggled Shawn, who for some reason found his own nonsensical comment so funny that he doubled over with laughter.

"Okay, I'm starting to think that those doughnuts made some sort of impact on Shawn's brain. Like, they left a giant-sized hole there!" mused Marsha as she witnessed her brother's unending fit of giggles.

"I tell you, there's something to that doughnut hole theory, Marsha! I'm feeling great this morning, really zippy, but also sorta airy-headed. Do you think it's all that sugar we had yesterday? Or maybe the trans fats?" asked Philo. "An unhealthy diet combined with going down into a cave again?"

Frank giggled, but at what he wasn't sure. "I feel weird, too, but I thought it was all that driving I did yesterday," said Frank, shaking his head as if trying to dislodge some internal cobwebs. "I mean, I feel great; I actually have that merry holiday feeling, but I feel weird too. Sorta fuzzy. I bet all we need is a nice long walk in the woods."

"Lead the way, Dad!" said Marsha and Shawn in unison, with Shawn using the hem of his tee shirt to dab at the tears springing from the corners of his eyes.

The group hefted their packs onto their backs and started for the trailhead. They had just reached the big wooden sign that had info about some of the flora and fauna in the region and land use rules and regulations, when Frank decided he needed to double check that the truck was locked and that the back country permit was visible on the dash board. "You guys wait here while I look," he said, and the three teens all took off their packs and used them for seats. "Gosh, I won't be gone that long!" said Frank as he turned to walk the less than fifty yards back to the truck.

Shawn watched as his father walked across the dirt lot and around to the far side of the truck. Frank checked that the doors were indeed locked, and then he shaded his eyes from the slanting morning sun to peer through the windshield for the permit. "Apparently not there!" said Shawn to the others as he watched his father patting his pockets and looking perplexed. At last Frank reached into his left rear pants pocket, took out a pink piece of paper and then started patting his other pockets, apparently searching for his keys. Again he shielded his eyes to peer into the truck's interior and his shoulders dropped noticeably. "Uh-oh," said Shawn, "I think Dad's locked us out!"

Frank turned in their direction and looked at them beseechingly. Marsha stood up, felt her own pants pockets and went to her Father's rescue. "Good thing I've got the spare set!" she called. When she reached the truck, Marsha looked into her Dad's smiling but perplexed face. "Wow, Dad, that's not like you to lock the keys in the truck!"

Frank shrugged and held his hands out, palms up in a sign of surrender. "Yeah, weird, huh? I really think I'm suffering from DHS!" said Frank in wonderment.

"DHS?" asked a puzzled Marsha, "What's DHS?"

"Doughnut Hole Syndrome!" giggled her father. "There really does appear to be a hole as big as Texas in my head this morning!"

7 The Forest for the Trees

Once they were finally on their way, Frank, Marsha, and Shawn walked the two and a half miles of trail in next to no time with the always enthusiastic Philo in the lead. They found the little pile of stones that marked their turn off to the southeast without any difficulty. "Alright gang, this is where we head south. It's fairly well trampled; we shouldn't have any problem following the trail," said Frank.

Philo straightened his posture and gave his uncle a mock salute. "As long as we keep a look out for the cairns and keep an eye on the compass we should be just fine!" said Philo, trying to sound confident. Shawn and Marsha thought Philo was as smart as anyone they had ever met, even as smart as their dad, Frank. But Philo's knowledge of things outdoor oriented were based rather heavily on theory. Sure, Philo had once been a Boy Scout, but of the big city variety, and he had of course experienced that spectacular camping trip to Ladron Peak last

49

year with Shawn and Marsha. But although that was a grand adventure, it was really only one short weekend; one short weekend where Philo had accidentally led his cousins on a chase for fool's gold that had gotten them all hopelessly lost underground.

Shawn looked mischievous as he addressed his cousin. "Um, you do know how to read a compass, right?" said Shawn. "I mean, no offence, bro, but we don't want to get lost out here."

"Be nice, Shawn, I'm sure Philo can read a compass! And don't forget, Dad's got a GPS in his phone, right Dad?" commented Marsha, simultaneously sticking up for her cousin and keeping all the bases covered.

"Yep, that's right. Plus it's even fully charged and in my pocket! I won't be repeating my forgetful show from back at the trailhead," said Frank with a nervous chuckle.

"Okay," said Shawn, "I think I'm convinced. It just that this endless sea of trees is confusing. I know there's quite a variety, but it all looks like wood to me!"

The four of them continued walking in silence, enjoying hunting for the trail markers and making it a game to spot the next little pile of stones and head off in that direction. After a time, the trail got a little harder to see, with the grass growing thicker and with more underbrush covering the path. "Phew, it's starting to get warm out here. Even under these trees," said Marsha, pushing her damp bangs from her forehead with the back of her hand. "Can we stop for a bit? I could use some water." She dropped her pack onto the ground and sat. "How much further to where we're headed?"

"We're kind of there already," said Frank. "I mean, Mister, uh, what was that guy's name? Started with an 'S'?" Frank looked at the palm of his hand as if expecting to see the name written there. "Hmm… Anyway, the hunter who saw our Lingerling says it was just about half a day's walk along this trail to where he saw the creature. So we should all be on the lookout," said Frank, eyes scanning the area. "Jeez, I can't believe I've forgotten that guy's name. My brain still feels fuzzy. Fuzzier, even…"

"No offence, Dad, but you guys *always* seem a little bit fuzzy to me," said Marsha with a grin. "Truly, I'm not surprised that Shawn can't tell an oak tree from a pine tree, but we'd better make sure that someone keeps an eye out for the trail markers. We don't want everyone looking for the omomyid and then walking off and getting lost. Let's have a snack and some water and then march onward," said Marsha. "And Philo, I designate you to be the trail guide."

"Why me? You know what happened last summer when you all followed my lead!" said Philo, his forehead crinkled in a frown. The teenager distinctly remembered how lousy he felt when he realized that he had mistaken iron pyrite for real gold treasure. "Remember?"

Shawn put his arm around Philo's shoulder. "Yeah, Cuz, I remember! We had an extremely awesome time!" he said, sinking his teeth into the apple he held in his other hand.

***

Trudy was checking her email and doing a bit of internet surfing before she got down to business and opened up the Photoshop files that she had been working on. "Hunh, here's an article about the shooting star that we saw, Candy!" she said, patting the dog's yellow fur. "Says here it was probably some space junk, part of a defunct satellite, and it was seen from the west coast clear across Texas! Whaddya know? I wonder how I could work something like that into the Terra Taurus space tourism campaign… Something like, visit space before it crashes to Earth? See outer space in its natural habitat? Hmm. If it landed in Texas, I should give the family a call and tell them to keep their eyes peeled. Maybe they can bring me some actual souvenir space junk!" She reached for the phone and just as her hand touched the receiver it rang, causing Trudy to jump. She gave herself a moment to recover before picking up the receiver and pressing the green "send" button. Her voice was calm as she spoke into the mouthpiece. "Hello?"

The voice was familiar and cheerful. "Hi honey, hope I'm not disturbing your work! We're just taking a hiking break in these beautiful woods and thought we'd say hello and tell you about our adventures so far!" said Frank.

"No, you're not disturbing me. In fact, I haven't quite begun to work yet. I'm just doing a bit of casual research to ease my way into work mode. So tell me," she said, "*have* you had adventures yet?"

"Have we?! You wouldn't believe the doughnuts we ate yesterday!" said Frank with a chuckle. "We've all got extreme sugar hangovers."

"What, even Shawn? I thought he was immune to such things."

"Well, actually Shawn lost his doughnuts. Tossed most of them behind a tree yesterday. Ya know, he upchucked? So maybe his sugar dose was ultimately smaller. No, but you wouldn't believe it. These were giant Texas sized deep-fried delicacies and they have altered our brainwaves."

Trudy smiled at the thought of Shawn getting his comeuppance. "Wow, so Shawn does have a limit!" she laughed. Well, you sound pretty okay to me. A little holiday silly maybe, but that's not unusual for you on any given weekend. The phone's breaking up a bit. Before I lose you… Have you guys managed to sight your mystery critter yet?"

"No, as a matter of fact, we haven't seen any animals at all. Not even so much as a squirrel. Weird, really. But I guess it is kind of hot. Maybe they're all asleep. I'd kind of like to take a nap, too." Frank giggled wildly.

"Frank, are you sure those doughnuts weren't fermented? Or brandy-filled?" Trudy was starting to think with some satisfaction that she couldn't let her family out of her sight. They always became a little undisciplined.

"No, we're okay, we're just having fun. In that summer vacay mood. No more pencils, no more books, no more Trudy's..." sang Frank.

"Hang on a bit!" interrupted his wife, putting a tone of indignation into her voice. "Wow, you guys *are* silly. Now don't get carried away! I expect you to look after those kids. Do I have to put Philo in charge?"

"Marsha already did that. Philo, she wants to talk to you-ooo," sang Frank, holding the cell phone out for his nephew.

Trudy frowned as she listened to the distant transfer of the phone to Philo. "Oh dear, the phone's still breaking up. Just tell me, Philo, is your Uncle Frank alright?" said a mildly worried Trudy. "Pardon me for saying so, but he sounds drunk. What are you guys up to?"

"Oh, we're okay Aunt Trudy. We're all just a bit goofy today. We stopped off for the giant doughnuts yesterday and then went to a cavern called 'Inner Space'. It was fun, but I think Uncle Frank did too much driving and Shawn ate too much and got sick and Marsha and I are just enjoying ourselves and our meander through the woods."

"Okay, I guess that makes sense, but I'm hoping you're not just wandering around aimlessly, are you? I mean, you do have a trail, a map, a plan, something?"

"Oh don't worry Aunt Trudy, we're just fine. I'm sure the trail is around here somewhere…"

"What?!" said Trudy, alarmed.

"Kidding Auntie, just kidding! We're good, honest. Don't worry, talk soon, bye!" and he hung up.

Trudy stared into the receiver, unsure as to whether or not to phone back. "Candy, they sure did sound weird. Now I'm wishing they took you with them!" she said to the nonplussed dog before finally hanging up. "Oh dear… Maybe I should have tagged along. Darn it, I didn't even tell them about the space junk…"

***

Philo squinted up at the trees around him. He had been watching his feet for… how long? He didn't know. It seemed like only minutes, but maybe it was hours. He ached from sleeping on the ground. Why in the world had he even tried to sleep against that tree with the lumpy roots? The pack on his back contained not only a nice down-filled sleeping bag, but a self-inflating roll mat. So why the heck hadn't he used those? Philo vaguely remembered being awoken briefly by another of those shooting stars. Hadn't he? "Maybe that was the same one," he said aloud, making no sense, even to himself. Now the sun was much lower in the sky than the last time they had stopped walking. Philo stood still and looked behind him. "They?" he asked. "Oh yeah, the others. Just where is everyone?" Philo couldn't remember the last time anyone had said anything to him. "What is going on?" he said aloud to no one.

Philo shaded his eyes from the sun slanting through the gap in the trees. All day he'd been walking alone in a daze. And all yesterday too, he supposed. He knew he should feel frightened at the idea of being separated from the others, but for some reason he felt fine about it, calm and at ease. Happy even, aside from the scrapes, bruises and bug bites from stumbling about in the thorny underbrush and sleeping without bag or tent. Something told him he should feel concerned, worried even, but he couldn't muster even the slightest bit of fear. Philo looked in the direction that he had been walking. He was heading toward a clearing of sorts. There was something unusual about that gap there in the trees. There was a blackness to the surrounding branches. Philo couldn't remember what kind of trees were so black. "Look," Philo said aloud to no one, "those trees are black." He paused, thinking, and spoke again. "And the grass is black, too." A concentrated look came over Philo's face as he worked hard trying to figure out what this could possibly mean. His smile spread as a plausible thought occurred to him. "Has there been a fire here?" Philo stepped forward into the open area.

A swath of the forest was just plain missing; a big path wide enough for a couple of school buses to drive through side by side. The trees here were charred black and appeared to have been turned into charcoal and soot. Philo walked further, and the burnt wood crunched beneath his hiking boots creating small clouds of black dust that rose up at every step. "How funny this is!" he said aloud, "How odd. It smells like a summer barbeque!" Philo sniffed the air and smiled. "Mmm, I really should find the others and show this to them." He looked around, only half hoping to see them, but still wondering, "Where are the others?"

8 Fall Down, Go Boom

A noise in the underbrush beyond the clearing made Philo look up. He still had a feeling that he *should* be scared. Should be worried, or frightened, or terrified, or maybe even petrified. Here he was, alone in the woods, in Texas of all places, and he was lost. The sun appeared to be going down even though Philo had no idea where the day had gone, and there was some *thing* making a crackling sound in the bushes. Even so, Philo held onto his feeling of contentment, his sense that all was well. More than that, Philo felt that all was great. Fantastic and fun, in fact. Excitedly, Philo thought about the unseen thing making the sound.

"It might be a wildcat, or even better, a bear! What an adventure!" Philo shook his head. "Wait, that's not right. That's not supposed to sound like fun. Bears are not kittens; this is not a good thing." Philo rubbed his eyes with his fists. "What is wrong with my head? I can't think clearly." He shook his head again to try and clear it and grinned. "This is not sunshine and lollipops," he laughed, "this is lost and alone in the forest!" A new thought made Philo giggle even more. "Lost like Hansel and Gretel! ...Ooh, maybe there's a gingerbread house around here somewhere! Mmm... gingerbread! Yum!! No! Not yum, yikes! Jeez, get a grip, Philo!" he told himself. "What is with me?" He looked up expectantly as the sound of the mysterious approaching maybe-bear grew louder. But he was momentarily disappointed when it was only his cousin Marsha, emerging from between some pine trees looking wide-eyed and happy. "So, no bear," he said to her.

"Say, there you are, Philo. Bear? What bear?" she said looking around and smiling. "I wanted to show someone this beautiful leaf I found, but I couldn't find anyone. Not even a bear," she giggled. "Look, isn't it perfect? Totally symmetrical and just the most lovely shade of green. I'm thinking I'll paint my room this color when we get back home. Or maybe I'll paint my truck this color, or maybe I'll dye my hair..." She spoke casually to Philo as though they had only been apart for mere moments rather than overnight. "What do you think?"

"Marsha, what I think... is that something's wrong. Or maybe not wrong, exactly, but that something *should* be wrong, or should *feel* wrong. I dunno. I mean, I think I've been lost. I slept up next to a tree." Philo stopped speaking and looked at the leaf Marsha was holding out to him. Once again he seemed to forget the seriousness of the situation that he and his cousin found themselves in. "Wow, you're right Marsha, that is a beautiful

59

color. Green, I think you call it, right? We should show it to your dad and Shawn. Have you seen either of them lately?" he asked, absent-mindedly massaging the crick in his neck.

***

Shawn and his father were enjoying a leisurely stroll through the east Texas forest and talking in an abstract way about the cuteness of baby animals. They had been walking together nearly all day, meandering here and there and delighting in the sights and sounds of the forest when they spotted a funny little creature looking at them from a low tree branch. The animal had huge round iridescent eyes and though it appeared to be a fully grown adult, it was undeniably as cute as any baby mammal could be. It was the cuteness of the little creature that had inspired their conversation.

"Cuteness makes mommies care," said Frank, in a sweet voice that defied his doctoral degree. "That's why your mommy loved you and your sister the instant she saw you."

"And you didn't?" asked Shawn brusquely. "What, you didn't think we were cute?" He sounded genuinely hurt, as though he were nearly on the verge of tears.

His father rushed to comfort and reassure him. "Sure, Shawn, sure I did, at least in that human kind of way." He put his arm around his son's shoulders and smoothed Shawn's hair. "I mean, you kids weren't as cute as a kitten or puppy, but... Anyway it's different. For a guy, I mean. To male animals, ya know, mammals for the most part, other small squishy helpless animals are either competition for food, or are food themselves. But you and Marsha were *my* small squishy helpless animals, and so I wanted to protect you both. The masculine way of nurturing, I guess."

"So what about other people's babies? Are you saying you would rather eat them than protect them?" said Shawn, still looking at his father, but hoping for reassurance that this was not the case.

Frank stopped walking and kicked at a burnt pinecone lying on the ground. The odd object distracted him for a moment and he said, "What were we talking about?" Frank paused to look around and turned himself, pivoting, in a complete circle. "Where's Marsha and Philo? For that matter, where are we?"

Shawn looked up at the swath of open burnt ground that they were standing in. An area about ten yards wide and about ten times as long was charred and void of the trees that they had previously been walking through. "Hunh," said Shawn. "Dad, check out these trees. I mean, these trees are not trees. I mean, there are no trees here. What happened to the woods?" Shawn looked from one end of the burnt area to the other. "Oh look. There's Marsha. And Philo, too."

Frank waved to his daughter and nephew at the far end of the open area. "Hey, were you guys lost?" he called. Turning to Shawn he said in a quiet voice, "Or were we lost? Shawn, my head's not right. Didn't we see a tapir back there? No wait, not a tapir... what was it? Shawn, didn't we see a tarsier? Wasn't there just a cute little furry critter looking at us from a tree, just like that Mr. Shhh-something said?"

Philo and Marsha were walking toward them. They both had big stupid grins on their faces and Shawn noticed that Marsha was holding a small green something out to him. "Hey Sis, you got anything more substantial to eat than lettuce? I'm suddenly starving."

Philo stepped forward. "No," he said, "I mean, look. Shawn, Frank, something's not right here." He was struggling to stay on topic; struggling to sound concerned. "This burnt area. It's weird. And my head. Feels fuzzy." Philo turned back to Marsha and gave her hand a shove. "Would you knock it off with that leaf? Yes, it's a lovely shade of green. But think. Marsha, how did we get here? What are we here for? I think we've been lost. Maybe we still are."

Frank spoke up, not sounding terribly concerned, but rather puzzled and amused, as though being lost in the woods were a huge joke. "Yeah, I don't know how long we've been wandering! Didn't we, I mean, we slept, didn't we? Or slept-walked?" He laughed and looked at his feet on the burnt earth. "I dunno where we are, but, hang on a minute... Shawn, I'm thinking you and I just saw what looked like our Lingerling! Or did we just dream it? Shawn?"

Shawn stroked his chin and looked down at the burnt ground. "No, Dad, I'm sure we saw something. I'm pretty sure we don't dream alike," said Shawn, "do we?" He turned to Marsha, who had picked up the leaf Philo had knocked from her hand and was studying it again. "Wait. How did you both get here? Weren't *you* guys the ones who were lost? Where's the trail? Where're your packs? You know, with the food?" Shawn turned himself around in a circle several times trying to see the pack on his own back. Finally he reached up to touch the straps that were still around his shoulders and breathed a sigh of relief. "Phew, still there!"

Frank sat down on the charred earth and held his head in his hands as if trying to contain his thoughts between his palms. His eyes were closed beneath his heavily furrowed brow. "We need to figure out what's going on here. If we concentrate, really hard, concentrate really hard..." He was silent for a moment and then he said, as though reciting a to-do list, "I know that we've been wandering around in a daze. I think we got separated; I think we got lost. But we all wound up here, at this burnt place. I think Shawn and I saw our creature, our Lingerling." Frank was trying hard to keep his thoughts on track; every word was taking his full concentration. "We saw the omomyid. It did look like a tarsier, but a tarsier wouldn't be here. How could a tarsier be here?" Frank looked up at his son and daughter. All three of the teens were looking down at Frank, but Shawn and Marsha had strange expressions of

63

incomprehension on their faces. Only Philo looked as though he was capable of speaking the same language as Frank.

"So what you're saying, Uncle Frank," said Philo pausing before each word, "is that somewhere around here is our Lingerling, our living fossil?"

Frank nodded with some difficulty as if hearing a question, then comprehending it, and then finally answering it required enormous strength. "Yes, I'm pretty sure that it is *actually* here, really here. But, where *here* is... that I'm not so sure about. I know that we got off the trail. Obviously we did. I know we've been wandering around for... a while, a few hours? Look. The sun is going down. It must be near dinner time."

"Wait!" said Philo as if struck by an amazing idea, "I have a watch!" He stuck out his wrist and looked at the thing strapped to it. "Hmm, numbers," he said, perplexed. "Here, Uncle Frank, you look."

Frank stood up and leaned in towards Philo. "Looks like six fifteen. Yep, we lost some time. Lost some time, that's funny." He laughed as if he had made a good joke. "Hey, if I can read a watch, who's to say I can't understand that map thingy?" Frank fished in his pocket for his phone with the GPS app and slid it open. "Okay, well, that's meaningless. I don't suppose it matters much where we are anyway. I mean, we really only need to get back to where we were. It's where we were that matters." Frank's face took on a quizzical expression again. "No that's not right." Frank looked up and saw that Marsha and Shawn had lost interest in the conversation and had wandered off. Frank knew that he shouldn't let them out of his sight, but for the life of him, he couldn't think of why.

***

Shawn walked around in a circle of increasing circumference as he listened to the abstract sound of his father's voice. He was enjoying watching the way the black soot puffed up from the ground as he took first one step, then another, then another. His brown hiking boots were becoming blackened, and Shawn was admiring the color change, thinking it an improvement, when he noticed that his left foot had started to slide down a steep incline. What followed was not only Shawn's right foot, but the rest of him as well and he smacked down hard onto his bottom and slid with a bump, landing next to a large round object that appeared to be charred and blackened like the rest of the surroundings.

Marsha looked up at the sound of her brother's tumble, and what she saw from her vantage point made her laugh loudly. She shouted over to Philo and Frank and pointed at where her brother had been standing. "Shawn fall down, go boom!" she said, giggling uproariously.

9 Some Nut

When Shawn looked up from where he lay, covered in soot and sprawled in a large indentation in the forest floor, he was surprised to see sitting next to him what looked like a giant burnt chestnut. "Ha!" he laughed, "I have been transported as a miniature to a yuletide hearth!" He had just started to sing the chorus to some old Christmas song, "chestnuts roasting on an open fire," as his sister appeared at the edge of the little valley, looking down on the strange scene. Hearing Shawn sing a holiday carol made her giggle even more than witnessing his tumble.

"Wow, Shawn, you look like you fell into a big black bowl," she said. The area where Shawn sat was indeed bowl shaped, and burnt like the path in the forest leading up to it. Her brother lay in the bottom of the little valley, half sitting with his back resting on a large spherical object that seemed to be partially buried or imbedded in the ground.

"Look, Marsha," he said gleefully, his face smudged with soot, "I found a big nut!" and he rapped at the object with his knuckles creating a hollow wooden sound.

"Well, that's weird," she said, "I see two of them. Big nuts, I mean." She climbed down the small incline to get a closer look. "Yep, that's a nut alright," she said. "Looks like a giant chestnut, or a mammoth filbert. I didn't know they grew them so big. Trust the Texans, right Shawn? Big skies, big doughnuts, big nut-nuts." She was starting to walk around the thing, stretching her arms out wide to get some sort of measurement when Philo and Frank appeared at the edge of the crater and looked down in wonder.

"Jeepers, Marsha, what's that you're hugging?" asked Philo, seeing his cousin with her cheek pressed against the object, trying to get her arms around it.

She looked up at Philo, cheek, arms and chest covered with the black soot. "I dunno, some kind of nut, I think. And I wasn't hugging it, I was..." She left the sentence hanging, not quite sure what she was doing to it.

"Wow," said Frank climbing down. "That's a pretty impressive...um...thing. What do you suppose it is?" he asked. He touched the side of the large round object and wiped off some of the soot onto his finger. "Ha! It does resemble a nut. A giant burnt nut. Or at least, it seems to be made of wood." Frank rapped on it with his knuckles, like Shawn had done, creating a hollow echoing sort of sound, and then he began to walk around it, like Marsha had done, stretching his arms wide. The object appeared to be about nine or ten feet in diameter, rising about four feet out of the ground with some unknown percentage buried in the blackened earth. "Philo," he called up to his nephew, "whaddya make of this thing?"

Philo jumped down, nearly crushing Shawn's hand, who still sat with his back leaning up against the nut-like thing. "Sorry, bro, you okay? Did I step on you? Shawn? Earth to Shawn! Ooh wee ooh," he said trying to rouse him with a weird theremin-like noise. "Are you gonna get up and let us have a look at this thing?"

Shawn stared up at his cousin with a goofy look on his face and started to giggle; a silly wet your pants kind of laugh. "Yeah," he sputtered, "I'm getting up, cause something is tickling my behind!" He jumped up and gazed down at the spot where he had been sitting. The black soil next to the strange object was moving, as though something was digging its way out of the ground. "Look, guys, something's coming out!" said Shawn as a small dirt covered face appeared, wide iridescent eyes blinking the soil away from its lids. The creature had a round face of a tawny grey colored fur and two pointed ears sat wide upon its head. It had a small nose and a mouth with thin lips that were set in an odd smirking expression. It was the eyes of the creature that were its most remarkable feature, large, round amber colored eyes that appeared to be almost glowing. "What the what!?" exclaimed Shawn. "Hey look! It's our Lingerling;

it's the critter we came looking for! We found you! Gee little guy, that's some nut you're trying to bury!"

Marsha and her father rushed around from the other side of the strange object and joined Shawn and Philo in staring down at the little creature. "Wow," said Frank, kneeling down with a big grin on his face, "that sure does look like the animal that Mr. Shepherd described." Realizing what he just said, Frank sat back on his heels and looked up at the three teens standing around him. "Hey," he said, "I remember that guy's name. Is it possible my head may finally be clearing? Two plus two is four, four plus four is eight, the atomic weight of hydrogen is one point zero zero seven nine four. If I only had a brain... Whew! At last!"

Frank signaled to the others to remain motionless as he crouched down lower to get a better look at the small furry animal that was still sitting where it had emerged from the ground. The creature seemed to take little notice of their presence as it sat, methodically picking the soil and soot from its pelt with its long thin fingers. Frank was conscious of trying not to frighten the animal, but the thing seemed to be wholly unafraid as it turned toward Frank, huge eyes blinking slowly, and looked intently into his face. Frank was instantly taken aback by the strangely direct gaze and the intelligent look in the creature's eyes as he spoke softly to it. "Well, let's see, my friend, are you a misplaced tarsier, or are you really some sort of Lingerling; an actual fossil come back to life?" So intelligent was the look on the little creature's face that Frank almost expected it to reply. "Did we find you? Or did you find us?"

Peering over Frank's shoulder, Shawn whispered, "Dad, didn't we see another one of these creatures when we were out wandering around? I vaguely remember that we were lost, weren't we? And we saw a little critter just like this." The creature looked up at Shawn and blinked slowly, as if it were affirming and encouraging Shawn's comment. Shawn tilted his head slightly to one side and considered the animal for a moment before addressing it. "Yeah, we saw your friend," he said. "But I'm afraid I can't tell you exactly where it was. We were all walking around in a fog. But I'm feeling clearer now." He paused for a moment before asking the creature a question. "You're here looking for others like you?" The creature blinked again, slowly lowering its lids over its glowing eyes and keeping them closed for a moment before opening them wide. Shawn tilted his head to the other side and spoke softly to the small animal. "Sure, we can help you find them. My dad and I saw one of your comrades, I'm sure we can find him again. Now that the fog has lifted."

Marsha, Philo, and Frank looked at each other with bemused expressions. Shawn the jokester, pretending to be carrying on a conversation with this weird little primate. "Um, Shawn," said Philo, speaking whilst trying to suppress laughter, "what're you doing?"

"You heard her, she's come here looking for the others. I'm just telling her we'll help," said Shawn, seemingly in all seriousness. "I mean, we will, won't we? We're not going to turn down a traveler in distress?"

10 Communication

Trudy was finishing up her work for the day, saving what she had done as pdfs and jpegs and other various formats, both onto her hard drive and on two small flash drives. A couple of years ago she had accidentally "lost" some promotional material that she had been slaving over for a local charity event when a can of cola was tipped onto the computer. The all-night Photoshop session that she was subsequently forced to put in saved the charity's yearly budget, but nearly killed Trudy. Since the "cola incident" as the family called it, Trudy was obsessive about backing stuff up. Overly obsessive. "Better safe than sorry, my dear doggie," she said, addressing Candy who as usual was laying close by.

As she logged off and shut down, she spoke aloud, "I think I'll try calling my family. See what they are up to. They sure sounded weird the last time we spoke." She got up from the desk and walked over to the big wooden salad bowl near the front door where the keys and cell phones lived when they weren't in purses and pockets. There was only one phone and one set of keys in the bowl, making Trudy feel a slight twinge of loneliness. She slid open the phone and pressed the send button, knowing that the last phone call she made had been to her husband. As she listened to the sound of the ringing phone, she only mildly wondered why no one picked up. When the thing went to Frank's voice mail account, Trudy sighed, figuring that he had let the battery run out, or more likely, that Shawn had been playing some games on the thing and had run the battery out for him. "Ah well, Candy, just the old ladies, home alone." Trudy returned the cell phone to the wooden bowl and decided to take a nice long shower.

***

Frank, Marsha and Philo, mouths hanging open, followed Shawn up and out of the little black crater. The Lingerling, or whatever it was, was perched on Shawn's shoulder, its long toes gripping his shirt and its long tail trailing down Shawn's back. "Okay, gang," he said authoritatively, "let's collect our packs, have a bite to eat and go help our new friend here find the others."

Marsha's gob-smacked expression changed to a frown as she spoke to her brother. "Seriously, Shawn, are you expecting us to believe that you are talking to that little squirrel?" she asked. "Aren't you worried about catching rabies or something?"

Shawn considered his sister. "C'mon Marsha, you know she's not a squirrel. Not even remotely. She says she likes the name Lingerling, but not for herself. More for the, um, old ones that they came here looking for."

"Oooh-kay," said Marsha, drawing out the word. "Maybe I wasn't really that far off about the rabies. I mean, my mind feels much clearer now, but you still sound way off balance! What would you say to a nice little nap, Shawn?"

Shawn ignored his sister's comment and looked into the large eyes of the creature perched on his shoulder. It blinked in the same slow way as before and looked back at Shawn. "She says she's been calling to the others, and maybe that's what made us all go goofy in the head. But she says it's probably what led us all to her."

"Ya know," said Frank, trying to make sense of his son's odd behavior, "I was just reading an interesting article about tarsiers before we came out here. We zoologists had thought that they were silent creatures, but it turns out they make sounds that are just too high of a pitch for humans to hear."

"Oh, are you trying to tell us, Uncle Frank, that a tarsier's silent calls confuse human brain waves? Or are you saying that Shawn has special hearing attuned to tarsier frequency? Neither makes sense, really... Oh, and that Shawn can hear *and* translate what they're saying as well? Hmm..." Just like the others, Philo was feeling much more like his old clear thinking self, but he was having a hard time believing that Shawn wasn't just trying to mess with him again by playing some joke. And now Frank was playing along, throwing in his jokester two cents. Philo shook his head slowly as he dug the toe of his boot into the ground thinking about all the times he had fallen for one of their jokes and ended up feeling the fool. Shawn really must have been preparing for this prank though, because it sure was fantastic. Philo looked up at Shawn with the creature perched on his shoulder and he said, "Okay, if that creature is talking to you, I find it hard to believe she said 'goofy in the head'? Strange choice of words for a wild animal!"

"Nah," replied Shawn, "I'm paraphrasing. She doesn't really speak to me in words. It's not even pictures. It's more like thoughts. And it's definitely not high pitched squeaks or squeals. I was the one who said 'goofy', not her. She's far too smart for that."

Philo shook his head. "C'mon, Shawn, stop pullin' our collective legs... But for the sake of the joke, let's have it your way. Let's assume for a moment that this weird little out-of-its-natural-habitat tarsier *is* talking to you. Although why I am playing along is beyond me. I guess I am that kind of sucker." Philo turned his face up towards the treetops and clasped his hands together behind his back, assuming the posture of a lawyer in a court room. "In the interest of having some fun, you say there are others. I mean you say that *she* says it; she says she's looking

75

for others. You and Uncle Frank did say that you saw another one, didn't you? What does this one say about that other one? Is it the one she's looking for? I mean who is looking for whom? I thought we were looking for a Lingerling, and now the Lingerling is looking for other Lingerlings." Philo frowned as he considered the concept that Shawn really was communicating with the animal. Even if it was just an ordinary tarsier, it was only a distant relative of humans and its brain wouldn't be much bigger than one of its eyes. How could Shawn possibly talk with it? "And why," Philo wondered, "am I even considering that it's possible that he really is?"

Shawn paused for a moment, looking once again into the eyes of the creature. They all watched as Shawn raised his eyebrows in a look of surprise, and then crumpled them into a look of concern. He was about to speak, when Frank spoke up. "Listen, Gang, I think we need to regroup. We are tired. We are lost. But we're thinking more clearly now. So let's act like it." He looked directly at Shawn. "We need a plan. And I don't mean some Shawn-type plan, no offence, where we go wandering off looking for more tarsiers. It makes no sense. Obviously this little guy, or sorry, *girl*," said Frank in response to a funny look from Shawn, "is the same one we saw yesterday. The very idea that there are more of these out here, based on the supposedly translated hearsay of a small cute primate, makes no sense." Frank frowned at Shawn who appeared to be deep in imaginary conversation with the animal, and stroked his own stubbly chin. "My beard says we've been out here for two days. Who knows how far we've wandered. My stomach says I've been ignoring it, so let's eat some food and get our bearings. We may want to just pitch camp here and settle in for the night. Get some rest. Start back in the morning."

"Phew, thanks Dad," said Marsha, "I sure am glad you're thinking clearly again. Glad we all are." She looked at Shawn, who was still gazing into the eyes of the tarsier and frowned. "Well, almost all of us," she said. "My pack is just over there. I really don't know what's in it in the way of food, but I'm suddenly very hungry. Whaddya say, guys? Dinner and a good night's rest? A comfy one with sleeping bags and roll mats?"

Philo nodded happily. "Sounds good," he said, relaxing his shoulders. "I think my pack is over there," he said, pointing to the far side of the burned and blackened clearing. Now that Philo's thoughts were once again his own, he couldn't help but start wondering about this strange burnt area of the forest and the even stranger giant nut that they found there. "Just how does this tarsier fit into all of this?" he said quietly to himself. Sighing, he added in a murmur, "I think I'll think about that later," as he headed off to retrieve his gear. "Eat first, think later."

***

The next morning Marsha awoke feeling more sober and clear thinking than she had at any time during the previous couple of days. She was the first one of the little expedition group to wake up, and she crawled out of her tiny one-person pup tent and looked at her father, brother and cousin, all sleeping peacefully in the open air and tucked snugly into their sleeping bags. She thought to herself that there must have been something really weird in those monster doughnuts that made them all feel so vacant and goofy; something that caused them all to lose their bearings and wander around in the woods imagining giant nuts and talking squirrels. Marsha stretched her arms up toward the sky and then down towards her toes in an effort to get the kinks out just as the sun was about to peek between the trees. Straightening up, Marsha was surprised to see a small furry face peeking out from Shawn's red sleeping bag. "Well," she said in a whisper, so as not to frighten the wild creature, "are you still here?" Marsha was even more surprised when an answer flooded into the front of her mind.

"Yes, naturally," the thought said, "you've promised to help us."

Marsha's eyes opened wide. It couldn't be. But it felt so real. Like the little tarsier was talking to her. Talking directly into her head.

"Yes, you can hear me now. That is good." The creature stayed looking out of Shawn's sleeping bag as it blinked slowly at Marsha with its strange iridescent eyes. "As I told your Shawn, it must have been my beacon call that interfered with your thought patterns." Again the thought-message came flooding into Marsha's mind, this time just like the last, as though it were a liquid being poured directly into her neurons. Marsha did not exactly hear the words; it was as though the words bypassed the mechanical structure of her inner ear and went straight to that part of the brain that turns sounds into comprehensible speech. Marsha shook her head, blinked, and rubbed her eyes as she looked at the small primate and heard… What? Its thoughts? "Perhaps something is amiss with my system," the thought-message continued, "My beacon should have brought the others. If they were in range, that is. It brought you all here, though. It is a benefit that the one called Shawn has agreed to help. He is your leader?"

Marsha laughed out loud as this last thought flowed into her. Now she knew she wasn't making it up. Even if her mind was playing tricks on her, it would never try to pull a joke like that. "Ha!" she exclaimed. "Shawn? Our leader? That's a laugh!"

At the sound of his name, Shawn tried to turn over inside his bag, but the tight fit of the mummy-style sleeping bag and the presence of a furry little animal caused him to awaken just enough to remember the odd events of the previous day and the incredible new personality he had encountered. He looked down into the face of the creature and spoke to it softly, saying, "I'm so glad it wasn't a dream."

11 The Pouches

"We came down in two pouches." The thought came into Marsha and Shawn's minds, appearing as a narrative, like a movie on a screen, but not in pictures exactly, not in words either, just in a kind of knowledge. Apparently this giant nut-like object was one of the things the creature spoke of, but beyond that, Marsha and Shawn had a difficult time saying exactly what she meant. "Pouch" was the best word that they could think of to translate the thought; "pouch" in the marsupial sense. Marsha and Shawn got the feeling that the creature was organically connected to the thing, but that it was also just a form of transportation, as though she was referring to something that was as much a city bus as it was a living womb. Apparently the creature was telling them that this giant nut was how she arrived here in this east Texas forest, but where had she come from?

They were all gathered around the strange blackened nut-like object as the little tarsier-like creature sat placidly on top and looked at them with her intelligent glowing eyes. Marsha and Shawn were standing, looking slightly down into the small crater while Philo and Frank examined the other side of the strange object. Marsha spoke, repeating the thought that she knew without a doubt came from the small furry primate-like being. "Apparently there are more of these things. She says they came down in them and I think she means, like, from another planet!"

"Let me get this straight," said Frank, "Now you both think you are hearing this little tarsier's thoughts? And you are trying to tell me that this creature is from outer space?" He spoke haltingly, trying to recite the supposed "facts" that his children were supposedly translating. "An alien from another planet? Came all the way here to east Texas? Looking for more aliens? Well." He bent down as he said this trying to get a glimpse of the underside of the blackened hunk of wood. Frank's mind felt totally clear this morning, all of the previous day's fuzz and confusion gone like it had never happened. Marsha and Shawn had explained to Philo and him that it was this creature's locator beacon that had caused the mental interference, like radio waves getting messed up when too near a power source. Frank thought the explanation plausible, except the part about, well, all of it. Telepathic tarsiers from space, travelling in giant wooden nuts. Frank certainly felt clear-headed, so what was wrong with his kids?

"Dad, I couldn't make this up! You know it's gotta be true if Marsha's in on it; she no lie," said Shawn. "I mean, test us if you don't believe it. I'll go behind a tree or something and we'll have her say something to Marsha and I and we'll each write it down. You'll see that we'll be receiving the same message."

"Shawn, you won't need to hide behind a tree," said his sister. "Just turn your back so that you can't see what I'm writing. We trust you!"

"Nope, the tree is *absolutely* necessary, 'cause I gotta go… if you know what I mean!" Shawn took off, laughing, for a not too distant clump of laurel oaks.

"Your Shawn is leaving?" came the creature's thought to Marsha.

"Oh, he'll be back," Marsha replied aloud, "He's just gone to attend to some, um, personal business." She felt silly talking about Shawn's need to relieve himself to a being from another planet. "So tell us…um, do you have a name?" She had to wait only a split second for the answer. "Dadive? Your name is Dadive?" An affirmative thought appeared in Marsha's mind and she continued. "Tell us, is this thing," she said, gesturing to the weird blackened nut, "your… um, pouch, is it a… space craft? How many of these came here, came to Earth, to look for the Lingerlings?"

A thought came back by way of reply. "Lingerlings seems a fitting name if you are referring to our ancestors of before…. But this time, two pouches were sent. This pouch that is here before you and one other. They were sent here, yes, to look for our Lingerlings. The other pouch came some short time ago, but communication was lost. So we came. It was the other pouch that I was calling to with my beacon. Something went wrong when we landed. Some calculation was off. Our pouch landed hard. I believe the other pouch did not make it." The thought came to Marsha as indisputable fact, even though the creature named Dadive did not know for sure the fate of the other pouch or of the creature it carried. It was an odd feeling for Marsha that the creature did not seem distressed by the possibility that she was the only one of her kind on Earth.

"Now wait," said Marsha, making a realization, "you said *our* pouch. How many of you were travelling in this craft? Are there more around here like you?"

Shawn appeared back at the edge of the shallow crater. Apparently Dadive's thoughts had continued to reach him while he was off in the trees, and he spoke aloud to the creature, "We saw another creature like you. Dad and I did. When we were, um, lost. I'm sure we did. Dad, do you remember which direction it was?"

Frank looked at his son and weighed the options. Both Marsha and Shawn seemed so natural and unphased about holding a half telepathic and half verbal discussion with this tarsier. Shawn was one to pull any kind of prank, inappropriate or not, but Marsha? She was a dreadful liar and would always spill the beans on any joke she was supposed to be in on. But what if they were both still suffering from the weird brain fog? Frank decided to go along with the gag, just in case. "Well, I *think* we did, that is, I'm pretty sure. We came into this clearing from back over there," he said, pointing to the southwest, "so I guess we could look in that direction. Although, we were very confused. Maybe we just saw this, um, tarsier twice."

"Hey, check it out. What's this?" asked Philo. He had been quiet all morning absorbing the situation and processing what his cousins were telling him. Not content to just believe what Shawn and Marsha were saying, Philo had been using a flat rock to dig around the bottom of the object, toiling away, trying to excavate some of the thing in hopes of finding some evidence, pro or con. "Wow, wouldya look at this!" he said in an excited tone. "Wow!" What Philo had uncovered not only confirmed that Shawn and Marsha had been truthful about the little primate, it also showed that this wasn't just some freakishly gigantic nut. "Look, Uncle Frank, they're telling the truth. There's a door buried down here; a sort of a hatch. It's a bit busted up." They all scurried around to where Philo was kneeling in the blackened soil, except for the unusual creature, who remained sitting atop the pouch with a peaceful expression on her little face.

"Can you pry it open a bit more?" asked Frank. "Hang on, I think there's a fold-up shovel in my pack. I'll go fetch it." Frank didn't want to leave them, even if it was only to walk the twenty yards to get his backpack. He wasn't sure what he was worried about; whether it was for fear of a reoccurrence of the brain fog, or fear that they'd get the thing open in his short absence and some sort of outer space monster would emerge and devour the three teens. Trudy would never forgive him. "Okay, Frank," he thought, "now you're starting to sound like Shawn. Outer space monster, indeed. Next thing, you'll be worried about Bigfoot. Jeez, how am I going to explain this all to Trudy? Telling her we found Bigfoot might actually be easier." Frank opened his pack and dug out the little metal folding shovel, removing the roll of toilet paper that was ensconced on the handle and stuffing it back in his bag. He turned to go back and the others were frantically calling to him.

"Hurry, Dad, we need to pry it open! We think there might be something alive inside!" shouted Shawn. The teens could hear a rhythmic sound of air moving, in and out, like the sound of breathing. The door, or hatch, was open just a few inches and had probably been enough space for the creature named Dadive to squeeze through, but it seemed as though she had left someone inside. They each strained to hear; Marsha put her ear next to the gap, and shushed the others to be silent. Dadive, the supposed space traveler, remained sitting placidly on top of the thing, apparently unconcerned with their activity, and not communicating with either Shawn or Marsha. Shawn considered the creature for a moment before addressing her with a direct question. "What's inside?" he asked simply. When the answer came flooding into his brain, Marsha stood up quickly with a shocked look on her face. She too had received the reply. Inside the pouch, apparently dying due to injuries suffered on impact, lay Dadive's traveling companion and mate, Wralis.

Marsha looked at Dadive and almost couldn't speak. Why hadn't the little animal with her oh-so-sweet face and large shining eyes mentioned that her partner lay dying inside the pouch? Marsha felt a cold shiver in spite of the increasing warmth of the east Texas morning sun flooding the clearing. This creature had travelled who knew how many millions of miles to this spot with her mate and now that he lay dying, she appeared unconcerned. Marsha spoke at last, one short question looking straight into the alien eyes. "Don't you care?"

"These are the risks we take," came the reply. The creature shifted her weight in order to casually scratch at one of her ears. "It cannot be helped. Wralis cannot be helped by us."

"We'll see about that," said Shawn as he grabbed the shovel from his father's hands and started digging frantically, removing the soil near the hatch, trying to excavate a larger area before prying it open.

Frank and Philo looked at each other, not comprehending what was going on. They had only heard half of the conversation, just Shawn and Marsha's questions, without knowing any of Dadive's answers. "Gee," said Frank, mystified, "what'd we miss?"

12 Inside the Pouch

Frank was astounded at the apparent biological similarities between the creature called Wralis that lay before him and so many other small but nameless primates that he had worked with at the BioPark. If Frank hadn't seen the interior of the strange space vehicle with his own two eyes, if he hadn't lifted out of it the fleshy green sleeping bag-like pod that contained the barely alive body of the little animal, he would have thought Wralis came from some sub-tropical forest rather than outer space. If Frank hadn't seen the instrument panel of the so-called pouch, made of what appeared to be wood, like the dashboard of a seventies' era station wagon, combined with a fluid gaseous ether, he would have thought that this little mammal was just a species of small tarsier-like primate that he hadn't encountered before.

Frank's first task was to assess the animal's injuries, assess the damage made by the impact of the semi-crash landing and see what he could do about it. Nevertheless, Frank's mind couldn't stop racing; reviewing what he had glimpsed of the inside of the little craft that they had removed this tiny being from. Gingerly, Frank had tried to lift the creature out, surprised when the little green pod he was sitting in detached and came out with him. The pod, like the fleshy leaf of a succulent plant crossed with a bean bag chair, cradled the injured space traveler as Frank laid him on the forest floor. Wralis, known to the other as mate and copilot, was in bad shape, unconscious and barely breathing with a pulse incredibly slow for a creature with a normally rapid heartbeat. Or at least what Frank supposed to be normal. Frank didn't think he could do anything to help the animal. He sighed and stood up, shaking his head and frowning. "I don't think anything can be done," he said sadly.

Marsha, angry and confused, was still glaring at Dadive as the creature sat, calmly perched on top of the nut-like spacecraft. The animal seemed unconcerned about the state of her mate, while Shawn and Philo marveled at the interior of the ship. The space inside was small and the hatch, finally pried open as far as it would go, only provided enough room for one of them to look inside at a time. They were told by Frank not to touch anything, but that didn't stop them from taking turns nudging each other out of the way in an attempt to get a better look.

"Jeez, wouldya look at that!" said Shawn in a whispered rush, peering in. Although he was concerned about the little alien, he couldn't contain his excitement about seeing the spacecraft's interior.

Philo sat back on his heels, finally giving in to his cousin. "Okay, Shawn, you win. I'll take my turn in a minute." Philo glanced over at the broken body of the passenger they had removed from the ship's interior. The small creature cradled in the green pod had stopped breathing, and Philo couldn't help but feel sad that the animal had made such an amazing journey only to expire here in the east Texas woods. "Where could these creatures possibly have come from?" he wondered. The space ship seemed real enough, although it was unlike any craft that had traveled from Earth to explore the galaxy, manned or unmanned. Philo examined the exterior again. Now that he had seen a bit of the inside, he could tell that this wasn't really a giant nut. The hatch that they had pried open mirrored the shape of the ship, being sort of a rounded trapezoidal shape and although it did appear to be made of some sort of wood-like material, something resembling a pecan shell, beneath the dust and soot it had a lustrous finish and revealed very fine seams. Philo could tell from the seams that the space craft had actually been assembled rather than grown on a giant tree but he had no idea how the thing could have been put together; there didn't appear to be any rivets or hinges or screws or anything.

Shawn had been making respectfully quiet little "ooh" and "aah" sounds during Philo's examination of the exterior. "C'mon, Shawn, describe what you see," Philo requested of his cousin. "Make some intelligent noises, wouldya?"

Shawn's voice came with a small echo from where his head was pressed into the little doorway. "It's kinda hard to describe."

Marsha grimaced, her face showing how upset she was about the creature's apparent death and how irked she felt about her brother's light-heartedness. "Try," she said flatly.

"Weeellll," Shawn drawled, "it looks like everything is made of wood, but it also looks like things are, um, made of smoke, or clouds. Little glowing clouds. Like if you took Dad's old wood grained stereo and threw it on a fire and watched it burn, saw the smoke and watched it glow, but without there being any flames."

Frank frowned at the mere mention of throwing his beloved eighties era turn-table on a pyre. "Let me have a quick look, Shawn. Then I really think we've got to bury this little guy."

Philo was about to complain about losing his place in line to have a look inside the weird space craft when he glanced at the small dead animal and picked up the shovel instead. "It's okay, Uncle Frank, I'll bury him." He walked off some distance, out of the burned area, to a small stand of laurel oak trees. Finding a spot between some large roots, he began to dig. He told himself he should mark the burial place with a rock or something, knowing that it might be desirable to locate the body again. "We just might need proof that we've been visited by aliens," he said quietly to himself.

Philo hadn't been digging for more than five minutes when he figured that the hole would be large enough for the diminutive creature. "Hmm, I wish I had a box or something to put him in.

I guess there's a plastic bag in my backpack, but that hardly seems like a fitting burial shroud for an intergalactic space traveler. I guess we could leave him in that pea-pod thing." He walked slowly back to where the group was standing near the space vehicle, planning to retrieve the little body, and dragging the shovel along in the blackened soot on the ground.

When Philo arrived back, his Uncle Frank wasn't peering into the hatch as he had expected. Instead he was kneeling over the male tarsier, the one that Dadive had called Wralis, who was sitting up slightly and coughing little tiny coughs. Frank spoke to the approaching Philo. "Look, I can't understand it! ...But he's okay, well maybe not perfectly okay, but certainly far from dead! How 'bout that?" Frank and Shawn were smiling broadly but Marsha still looked at Dadive with a severe look on her face.

"You knew he'd be okay, didn't you? Why didn't you tell us? Why did you let us feel all sad and sorry?" she said pointedly at Dadive.

The answer flooded into Marsha and Shawn. "I have not met your kind before. I do not know in what ways we differ. I told you he could not be helped. I do not know what you mean by 'feeling sad and sorry'." Dadive's thought message paused, and the creature tilted her head from side to side as though studying the human teenagers. She continued, "It is what it is. Wralis was damaged, but now he is repairing. Apparently you do not share this capability for repair. Sometimes for us it works, sometimes it does not. I myself have been repaired several times. I believe

91

you call it healing." Dadive leapt down off of the ship to Wralis's side. The two looked at one other for a moment before Dadive's thoughts once again flowed into Shawn and Marsha's minds. "We will let Wralis recover for a little while longer, and then we must look for the other pouch, and perhaps the other pair of Explorers if they are still alive. You may help us if you like."

13 Searching

While the little creature Wralis rested, Dadive gave the group a bit of a tour around the interior of the ship. Dadive would pass thought-messages straight into Marsha and Shawn's minds and then Marsha would give Frank and Philo a verbal interpretation of what the creature said. "She says this is just a small part of the ship. Apparently this thing is like a pod that the main ship jettisons off of to send the, um, astronauts, I guess you'd call them, down to the surface of a planet," translated Marsha. Marsha looked perplexed for a moment, wondering how the creatures were supposed to get back to their main ship, wondering where it was, wondering how far they had travelled, wondering if these furry little creatures were indeed astronauts in the true sense, wondering if they had built the machines themselves, wondering so many things that Dadive jumped up on Marsha's shoulder and put one long fingered paw on

Marsha's forehead. The gesture had the effect of silencing the questions swirling about in Marsha's mind.

"Listen," said Dadive in Marsha's thoughts, "I will answer all of your questions. But in time. Slowly and in time. Like Wralis, our pouch may regenerate as well."

Marsha marveled at the little creature. When Dadive placed her tiny strange long fingered hand on her forehead, a feeling of calm peace came to her. Like a feeling of letting go of all of her cares and responsibilities. When Dadive touched her forehead, Marsha felt as though she were not only receiving a communication from Dadive, she was also receiving an emotion. Or more precisely, a lack of emotion. A peacefully empty feeling.

But then a new thought came to Marsha. Not from the little alien being, of this she was sure, but from her own mind. Perhaps she had wrongly perceived Dadive's calm attitude earlier as coldness. Maybe it hadn't been that Dadive didn't care about what happened to Wralis; maybe she just knew she had no power to help him, no responsibility to try to heal him. Most likely she knew that Wralis and the little nut shaped space pouch could fix themselves. Marsha frowned and thought, "But whenever I feel powerless to help, I feel *more* anxious, not less. How could not being able to help Wralis make Dadive appear not to care about him?"

It seemed to Marsha that these creatures had emotional intelligences that were different from the ones of humans. She wondered if they were they less empathetic, but it seemed odd to her that they could have telepathy without empathy. That they could send messages in and out of each other's brains, but didn't have emotional attachments to one another. Dadive at least, Marsha thought with a shiver of sudden coldness, had a different kind of emotional intelligence than she herself did. "Maybe," Marsha thought, trying to put the matter aside, "just maybe, I'm not used to getting messages from alien beings sent telepathically into my head!"

Shawn looked at her with a laugh and said, "Ya think?"

"What, did I say that out loud?" asked Marsha. She turned to her father with a look of panic on her face. "Did I, Dad?"

Frank looked at her with some confusion. "Did you what? I didn't hear anything. I mean, again. Okay, kids, I think I'm losing it or maybe I need hearing aids. This is like imagining that people are constantly whispering behind your back."

Shawn looked at his sister with interest. Then he decided to try an experiment. He thought to himself, "No, Marsha, you didn't say it out loud, but I heard it. Do you here this? Peter Piper picked a peck of boogers…"

Marsha suddenly gave her brother a disgusted look. "Oh, Shawn! Boogers!? Really?" she said with a squeal.

Philo and Frank looked at each other, more confused than ever. "Are you guys forgetting to translate something?" demanded Philo. "What is Dadive saying?!" Philo was understandably very excited about the little space-nut capsule and its occupants. He wanted to know all about where the creatures had come from, all about the wood-like material the craft was built from, all about the strange glowing clouds inside, all about the instruments made of green fleshy stuff, and so many other things. Being out of the conversational loop was driving him crazy.

"Sorry, Cuz," replied Shawn, "this is too weird! I think I'm getting telepathic messages from my sister! Do you know what it's like getting a peek into *her* head? Yikes!"

Marsha crossed her arms. "Shawn just transmitted an altered nursery rhyme into my mind. What an unbelievably horrible ability for such a boy. It's bad enough having to listen to him talk, but to hear him think? Ugh!"

"No, seriously? Are you two really able to communicate telepathically with each other?" asked Frank excitedly. "This is unbelievably awesome! Rub some off on your Dad would you? Jeez this would come in so handy at the zoo. Can you imagine how much easier it would be if you could ask an angry leopard where it hurts? If I could talk to the animals! I could truly be Dr. Doolittle!"

Marsha shot a telepathic thought to her brother. "Hey!" said Shawn out loud, "That's not nice! Dad, Marsha called me Dr. Doo-nothing! Wow, I did get that from her! Just like that old movie, 'Escape to Witch Mountain'! Messages from my creepy sister through thin air! You better watch out what you think, Marsh!" Shawn balled his hand up into a fist and playfully shook it at her.

A confused thought-message from Dadive interrupted Shawn and Marsha's playful banter. "I do not understand. You no longer wish to know about our space craft? Our voyage? You no longer offer your help to search for the others?"

Marsha snapped back instantly into the serious frame of mind that the little alien radiated. "No, no," said Marsha, "we truly are interested! Shawn and I were just playing."

A strange faraway look came over Dadive's wide-eyed face and it felt to Marsha like a cold steel shutter had just been closed inside her mind. When Marsha looked again into Dadive's eyes, the strange feeling of the shutter being opened, of a curtain being lifted came to both Shawn and Marsha and they each shivered as the creature once again began telling them about the space craft and what brought them on this journey. "Allow me to start at the beginning. We have time while Wralis rebuilds his health. I will tell you about our race and our history, especially the history that we share with your planet, and why we have come here."

Marsha translated all of this to Frank and Philo, leaving out the part about the strange and uneasy feeling of the closing and opening shutter in her head. She could sense that Shawn had experienced the same creepy feeling as well, and they exchanged an odd telepathic "me too."

Book Two – Far and Ago

1 Decay

"You all know these figures are correct; they have been checked and rechecked. Grendille will reach critical capacity at the start of the next sun cycle. Our ability to manufacture enough breathable air for everyone..." The scientist paused, letting his sentence hang, and adjusted his ear piece with his long gray-blue fingers. "Well. From then on," he continued gravely, "it will begin to be disastrous for... everyone."

The Lingerlings

The experts of all things environmental had gathered in the chamber of Grendille's highest office to share with the Grand Commission the latest statistics about the planet's health and population. The situation was not a surprise to those assembled. It was not the result of an unexpected natural disaster or some act of war that had been imposed on them from some other planet. This was history repeating itself; the scene was familiar ground. Indeed, everyone on Grendille, from the very young to the very old, had studied The Exodus in their primary education. Since they were small the inhabitants of this tiny planet had been infused with the stories of the great voyage and their arrival here.

All children knew of the pouches of Explorers that had been sent out into space, taking with them the hopes of the people that they find a new home before the complete death of their old one. Children all over Grendille were tucked into their sleeping pods each night with soft toy versions of the large eyed creature, nick-named Little Grendu, who had come back with the good news. This new home had been named for the little Explorer and most of the origin stories centered on fanciful versions of Little Grendu's adventures, the discovery of Grendille, and the subsequent relocation. It wasn't until the children had grown into young adults that they learned the real reason behind The Exodus.

Now, after all they knew, the situation was being repeated. The new planet was in decay, and the Explorers were again being sent out in pouches, searching for yet another planet that could

100

sustain the so-called necessary members of the population, and relieve the strain. Several of the pouches of Explorers were due back soon. The ships that would take teams of settlers, the farmers and builders, scientists and politicians, were ready to go should they bring good news with them.

Goris fidgeted in her chair and sighed uselessly as she tried to think of a way to spin the words she was hearing into something more hopeful. She had to keep telling herself that now was not the time to give up. "The pouches should start returning soon," she said. "We can only hope that at least one of them brings a favorable report. There must be at least one place out there that can sustain a colony. At least for a time." Goris tried to tamp down the anger that was rising inside of her. "Why, why, why," she asked herself, "why didn't we prepare sooner?"

The environmental biologist named Trillig turned to the gathered colleagues and dignitaries and addressed them in unusually frank terms. "If we don't get relief to Grendille soon, things will start to get very tough. For us, as well as for those already suffering. We should not have waited so long."

Goris had long ago tired of the usual polite protocol in the face of this huge disaster and she stood up abruptly. Shaking with anger she spoke in a rush, words tumbling out from her thin lips. "Shouldn't have waited so long?! Are you kidding me?!" She leant forward on the table in front of her, spreading out her long fingers and using them to support her slight frame. "Tell the truth! We should not even be in this situation! We should have learned from the mistakes of our ancestors and had the courage not to go down the same abusive channels of waste and greed that they did. It's shameful and deplorable. Part of me hopes that the Explorers *don't* return with anything like a livable alternative! I think the people of Grendille deserve what's coming to them!"

"Now, now, Goris," said her colleague, reaching out to pat her cold hand. "You know the fault does not lie entirely with the people!"

Goris' large dark eyes narrowed at Trillig. "What?"she sputtered, "Are we living on the same planet!? Trillig, if the people didn't cause this, then who? It is not the fault of anyone else and certainly not the Explorers. Now is not the time for us to hide behind pretty stories! We can't keep pinning our hopes on new stars. Truly, are we destined to travel around the known universe populating and then polluting and destroying planets? Just because we can, it doesn't mean we should!"

"Well, there's enough of them, isn't there?" Sarspec, Councilor to the Highest Office, posed the rhetorical question to the group at large. "I mean, lots of planets, we just need to find the right one. We are most fortunate that we still had any Explorers left to send out. No more in the wild, I understand. No more wild for them to be in, either," he chuckled. "Well, at least one of our number was thinking ahead by breeding those hideous but useful little beasts."

Goris spoke up again. Her blood was boiling with anger, flushing her cheeks a bright turquoise. "They are not hideous little beasts. Really, I wish I hadn't played a part in this whole thing! I hope the Explorers find a wonderful planet and stay there! Start their own colony in a place that won't be destroyed by the likes of us, where they can get back to living in the way of their ancestors! Trees, nature, life in the wild! Not kept locked in laboratory cages and sent hurtling through space in pouches!" Goris had been thinking these thoughts long before she began leading the breeding program of Explorers. She had wanted to save the wonderful creatures with their large eyes and long fingers, so much like her own, for the sake of the species and not just to send them off in pouches to correct the mistakes of the people. She had no way of putting the plan in motion, but she would often dream of discovering some way to send the little Explorers off to distant planets, not to return and save her and the others like her, but to start colonies of their own. She would imagine somehow tinkering with the bio-engineered pouches so that they would land safely, but wouldn't be able to return. Unfortunately, the pouches were off limits to her; even if she knew how to "fix" them, she couldn't get near them. The only small gesture that she could manage toward her dream was making sure that the little creatures were sent off in matched pairs of successful breeders.

***

"We'll be arriving back on Grendille soon if the calculations are correct." The small Explorer perched on the edge of her bio-engineered simulated wooden branch and surveyed the instrument panel. "Won't they be surprised?"

The two Explorers were in their pouch hurtling through space on their return voyage. Hundreds more of the small furry mammals had been sent out in other similar craft. Like a dandelion in the wind, larger ships broadcast the pouches and their occupants out into the universe in the hopes of finding a planet with suitably life sustaining conditions. The creatures had been bred for the distinct purpose of being test dummies, but Marna and Sparstie were different. Their journey had changed them. They knew that settlers of Grendille had done it again, that they had managed to mess up another planet with overuse and overpopulation and the little creatures they called Explorers were to be their rescuers.

A lot of the Explorers wouldn't return at all. The scientists, so desperate to find a new place to colonize, had extended the parameters of what might be safe and sacrificed the pouches and their occupants. It was just like the people of Grendille to be extravagantly wasteful of their resources; neither the conservation of manufactured or living things mattered. Many were the pouches of Explorers that met unpleasant ends out in the far reaches of the galaxy. Most that were going to return had already done so, and none with any particularly cheerful results. But Marna and Sparstie were going to be the exception. Not only were they returning alive, with their data collecting instruments full of good news about the perfect conditions of the planet that they had been sent to, but they also were returning with something else that they found there.

Goris was there in her official capacity as the head of the Explorer breeding program to take custody of the two Explorers once the pouch arrived safely and it was determined that the pair was alive. It would be Goris' task to evaluate their health and send her report that would be compared with the data from the pouch. This would be used to figure out the suitability of the planet that Marna and Sparstie had returned from.

Goris wheeled the two cages down the long white corridor to her laboratory. The two Explorers inside seemed to be quite frisky, in spite of the long voyage they had only just returned from. Goris looked at the pair, her large black eyes flitting from Marna to Sparstie as she wondered if they really were alright. Was the pair behaving normally? Goris had seen several pairs return from test voyages, both short and long, and they always appeared tired or nauseated. These two seemed healthy and excited. Or was it agitated?

Goris touched the control pad lightly with her long index finger, lifting the gaseous curtain that served as the door to her lab and she wheeled the cages inside. "Ah, to be home," she thought flatly. "Now what made me think that?" she asked aloud.

"Because you heard *me*," came her next thought. "It was not you who said that. It was I."

2 We Became

Goris stared in disbelief at the small furry mammal in the cage in front of her. "Yes, that's right, it was me. My name is Marna. You know that; it was you who named me. You were there at my birth; you have been with me nearly every day since." The Explorer blinked at the scientist in her gray tunic. "But you weren't with me during our voyage."

Goris stepped backward, away from the cages and their occupants. "No, I'm tired, I'm worried, I'm under way too much stress. I must visit the Soother. I need a vacation from this doomsday scenario." Goris shook her head and closed her eyes momentarily, trying to block out the laboratory in front of her and imagine a place of natural beauty and peace that she had never, in reality, known. The Soother had taught her the technique of imagining the blue fields of tranix flowers as a way to calm down when the stress got to her. "The planet that we were sent to was not unlike the scene you are creating in your mind." The phrase interrupted Goris' thoughts, shattering the peaceful image she was trying to summon.

She opened her eyes and stared at the Explorer, who now sat on top of her cage along with her mate. "We reached our destination. We saw the planet. We got out and looked and walked and climbed. It was a good place for us. We became." Goris continued to stare. The thoughts were coming from the female Explorer. The little animal with the large eyes and tawny fur and the hands with long fingers so much like her own. She was making the thoughts in Goris' mind; there was no doubt. "It is true. You see now. I am talking to you Goris. In your mind." The little creature paused and blinked luxuriously, letting it all sink in to Goris whose eyes were darting around the room as though looking for an alternate source for the strange thought-messages. "It's all right. It is good, in fact. You see, on this planet... The planet your kind numbered as three-oh-nine-bee... We became."

Goris was trying very hard to keep her composure. She was one of the premier experts on these creatures they had come to call Explorers because that was their function. She knew everything there was to know about them. Goris had always found them to be intelligent creatures, but this one... This one was seemingly sending telepathic messages in complete thought-sentences. "No, not possible," she thought. She took a deep breath and decided to give herself the benefit of the doubt. "Wha-wha-what do you mean you became?" she said aloud.

"We became aware, conscious, able to string together complex thoughts and understand complex concepts. Do you see? When we found ourselves on three-oh-nine-bee, it didn't take long for us to notice that something was different. The air was breathable, as the instruments indicated."

"Yes," said Goris aloud, "the door would have, at least theoretically, remained locked if the atmosphere was deadly, and the pouch would have just carried you back here." Goris wasn't too sure that that was entirely true. Many pouches had simply not returned and Goris had been present when pouches opened to reveal the bodies of Explorers that had died. Her own autopsies had shown that some deaths were due to having inhaled poisonous gases. Goris frowned and felt ashamed when the next thought-message from the large-eyed creature appeared in her mind.

"I understand. We are the lucky ones, then?" The creature named Marna used a hand-like foot to luxuriously scratch an ear. "After the hatch opened, we roamed around for a while, investigating the surroundings, smelling the new aromas, nibbling at the plants and other living things to see what was safe to eat. We found a water source, and drank. And then, we became."

Goris furrowed her brow. She couldn't believe it, and yet to believe the alternative, that she was losing her mind, was unthinkable. "So it was after you drank the water? Immediately after?" she said.

"We do not know for certain if that was the source of our awakening. We explored the plants, we breathed the atmosphere, we ran, we climbed, we ate, we drank." The thought message from Marna appeared like an idyllic glowing light inside Goris' head. If this beautiful planet, number three-oh-nine-bee, held some substance that caused consciousness, heightened awareness and gave telepathic powers to Explorers, what could it mean for the people of Grendille? Goris' mind was racing with the possibilities. Maybe the brutish thinking that had caused the near destruction of this, their second home planet, could be altered. The path of destruction across the Universe could be stopped. Perhaps the people of Grendille could move to three-oh-nine-bee, name it Marna after this wonderful creature, and be transformed into responsible caretakers of their new world. Couldn't they?

Goris considered the creatures before her. Maybe they still held the key to what had caused their transformation. "With your permission, I would like to examine the two of you. To determine the cause. With your permission, of course," she said to the Explorer.

"You ask for permission. That is a new thing. A good thing. You, Goris, have always shown respect to our kind." The Explorer lowered her head in a slight bow. "Permission is granted."

"But I must ask one question." Goris paused, composing herself. "Marna. Why? Why did you return? Why didn't you and Sparstie just stay there? Have children? Have a wonderful life?"

The reply came in a one word thought-message. "Duty."

***

Goris worked tirelessly around the clock, looking for anything out of the ordinary that could have caused the transformation in the Explorers. She placed an initial report that stated that the pair appeared to be in good health, but that effects of their exposure to planet three-oh-nine-bee needed further study. Goris kept her assistants at a distance, with the excuse of quarantine. She took hair samples, blood samples, urine and stool samples. She mapped brain waves and pulse rates, and scraped the plaque from their teeth. She looked at molecules and marrow, nail beds and iris scans.

She discovered that although the male Explorer, Sparstie, had the same level of conscious awareness as his mate, he apparently was not capable of telepathic communication with Goris and so they relied on Marna to translate for him. The pair would stare intently into each other's large amber colored eyes and then Marna would turn to Goris and a thought-message would flood into her mind. It was after four days of inconclusive tests that Sparstie suggested through Marna that Goris try to obtain some of the water, soil, air and plant samples brought back by their space pouch.

The scientist in charge of testing those samples was the environmental specialist who had been present at that last desperate Grand Commission Gathering. Trillig wasn't a bad sort, but he was just as short-sighted as the rest of the experts involved with the project of finding a new home planet. It had been Trillig who had initiated the intense urgency of the project, identifying that Grendille was close to the brink of instability. Goris was extremely distressed that the man hadn't said anything sooner, so that they could all begin working on a way to fix the situation before it became desperate, but perhaps by the time the scientist had identified the problem, it was too late. It seemed to Goris to be unlikely that the man could have been so blind to such a massive problem, but she had to think it possible because he would be the one she would have to talk to in order to get some of those samples. She would have to come up with a good excuse why she needed them. Maybe even the truth.

3 The Key

Trillig was walking down one of the long white corridors going over the figures in his head. The tests he had run on all of the samples that the pouch brought back from three-oh-nine-bee looked favorable. In fact, they looked extremely favorable. There was water, plentiful and pure, and an atmosphere that was better than Grendille's had been when it had first been colonized. The images that came back showed a beautiful landscape with flowering plants indicating that crops could be grown and potentially pollinated naturally. It had been generations since anything had been grown naturally on Grendille. Most food products were bio-engineered in labs, meat and vegetable matter alike created by manipulating DNA molecules. Three-oh-nine-bee could be a planet for fresh new beginnings, and it seemed to Trillig to be too good to be true. Was that why he felt so uneasy about three-oh-nine-bee?

Deep in thought about the origin of his feelings of apprehension, Trillig wasn't aware of anyone approaching from behind until he felt a tug on his tunic. "Hey," said Goris, slightly out of breath, "didn't you hear me calling you?" Goris had decided on using a friendly casual approach to try and get some samples from the environmental scientist, and so she smiled broadly at the startled looking scientist and tried to catch her breath. "Wow, you're right. Even the air quality in here isn't as good as it used to be."

Trillig looked up at his colleague and nodded. "Yes, the purifiers and scrubbers are having a harder time trying to keep even the interior of Grendille supplied with breathable air." He frowned as he said this, another reminder that something should have been done long ago, and now the push was on to find another home planet and three-oh-nine-bee seemed to be their one and only hope.

Goris smiled again, trying for a natural expression, and laughed nervously. "Um, so how are your test results from three-oh-nine-bee? The Explorers seem to be in great health. No ill effects that I can determine." She laughed nervously again. "Heh, heh, no affects at all. Healthy little critters. Looks like three-oh-nine-bee might be the place for us. What do you think?"

Trillig considered her for a moment. Why was she acting so nervous? True, lots of people were acting nervous these days. Everyone knew their days here on Grendille were numbered. Everyone knew it was time to go. But Goris wasn't usually one to show it, at least not with this weird girlish giggling. Except for her understandable outburst at the Commission Gathering, Trillig's biologist colleague was usually strictly business. Not cold towards him exactly, but not warm and fuzzy either. Goris had a reputation for being more emotionally attached to her work and the Explorers in her charge than to any other bipedal beings. Still there was that show of emotion at the Grand Commission Gathering. And it was mainly directed at him. It wasn't his fault this planet was dying; he was just the messenger. Maybe she wanted to apologize. "Look, Goris, I hope you're not going to apologize for what you said at the GCG."

Goris was confused. Her mind had been so focused on trying to find a way to get those samples. What *had* she said at that meeting? She couldn't think. "Um, nooo," she said trailing out the word. "I wasn't even thinking about it."

"Well, *I've* been thinking about it, and you're right. Something should have been done a long time ago. Long before we were ever born. And you know, I'm starting to think that we'll need to make some major changes to the leadership of Grendille…" He looked nervously over his shoulder. This kind of talk would not be welcome in the underground hallways of the Citadel of Science. Trillig shuffled nervously, lowered his voice and said, "I mean, look, Goris, can I talk to you in private? I've been doing some thinking. About what you said. And about what has become of Grendille and of what could become of three-oh-nine-bee. If we aren't careful."

114

Goris' black eyes opened wide. Trillig seemed different. "Could it be that he is more conscious?" the biologist thought to herself. "Was it really just what I said at the meeting? Or could it be that something in one of the samples from the pouch has heightened Trillig's awareness of the implications of our situation? If it could make the Explorers able to think and reflect..." Goris' mind raced at the thought that maybe three-oh-nine-bee could be colonized responsibly and not just be another planet on their path of destruction. "S-s-sure, let's go in my lab. It's right around the next bend."

***

The two scientists entered into the lab through the membrane of ether under the watchful eyes of the two Explorers. Trillig was startled to find that the creatures were not caged, but were instead allowed free range of the room. "Is this the pair that went to three-oh-nine-bee? Aren't you afraid that they will break something, or mess up your work, being allowed to roam around free like this? Shouldn't they be in a cage? " he asked.

Goris shot a quick look at Marna and held one long finger up to her thin lips to silence the mammal from sending a reply into Trillig's mind... "No, this pair are exceptionally well behaved," she said, smiling at her colleague while giving the female Explorer another look. "In fact, I have learned so much from this pair about their time on planet three-oh-nine-bee. Apparently it is a wonderful place. Perfect, perhaps. But, ahem, let me get to the point. There is something that I am curious about..."

Trillig interrupted, "No, let me get to the point. What you said at the Gathering. About us going around destroying planets. I don't know. It's like, I was looking at the samples that came back from three-oh-nine-bee, my findings were looking good; this planet looks so, well, beautiful, idyllic... And suddenly I saw that what you were saying, that we could just be following some sort of sick destiny by going around the universe, going from planet to planet to planet, through time..." His voice trailed off as the thought continued to take shape. Trillig looked at Goris, looked the biologist straight in the eye and said, "We could just be destroying the universe one planet at a time. Look at our history. We can't repeat it. We can't allow it to happen again."

Although Trillig wasn't aware, Marna and Sparstie were paying close attention to the words of the visitor. Marna was dying to speak. Leaping onto the slim shoulder of Goris, she placed one long fingered hand on the biologist's hair. Goris looked at her and nodded. Then the thought came to Trillig like water pouring from a faucet into his mind's eye: "It doesn't have to happen that way again. We can change things." Trillig looked up, puzzled. "We?" he said aloud.

"Yes," said Goris, unsure of how to reveal what she knew. "Yes, you and I. We can make our case to the Commission; let them know that things must be different this time. That we can't just

116

keep going around the universe using up the resources and leaving our waste behind on barren planets. This planet, three-oh-nine-bee, it's pristine. We can start anew. We can treat our new home with the respect it deserves."

"Do you realize what you're saying? You, we, whatever, we would be asking society to start over again. To totally rearrange our priorities. To use only what we need and replace what we use for the sake of future generations." Trillig threw up his hands in a sign of desperation. "There's no way anyone will go for that! It sounds treasonous!"

"Wait," said Goris, "there is a way." She took a deep breath and coughed. "There's something I've discovered. Something about planet three-oh-nine-bee. I think there's something special about this planet that holds the key to its own future well-being. Actually, I think we may be in possession of that key already."

Then a message appeared in Trillig's mind, again flowing like liquid into his thoughts. "Together, with your help, we can find it. The four of us… We can find it… The key that will save both of our species and will ensure that this terrible history is never repeated again."

Goris looked at Marna and Sparstie and smiled.

4 The Four of Us

Slowly but surely, Trillig was calming down and getting a mental grip on the situation. Goris and Marna had filled him in on what they knew about planet three-oh-nine-bee and the miraculous potential it held. Goris asserted that it was an effect of one of the samples that he had been analyzing that gave Trillig new found concern for the environmental fate of the soon to be colonized planet. It was her assumption that some substance brought back in the pouch, most likely the same stuff that caused Sparstie and Marna to become conscious and capable of communication had caused Trillig to have his consciousness raised as well.

"Look, Goris," said Trillig, "Remember that you are a scientist. I can see this is exciting, especially for you; to be communicating with your Explorers! But I think you might be confusing two different kinds of awareness. I mean, Sparstie and Marna had an increase of intellectual activity. They can think for themselves and communicate in a way that they never could before. But that doesn't mean that they also became more enlightened in regard to our, um, environmental difficulties. It doesn't mean that some foreign substance has caused me to see that our species needs to change direction. I'm sure I was feeling that we had to put a stop to our path of planetary destruction before *any* of the pouches came back. I'm sure of it. All of my research, all of the science, it points right to it."

"Perhaps you are right, but I still think that the potential for our species to become less wasteful and abusive of our resources hinges on having something change. I mean, some *vital*, some *organic* change must occur inside of each of us..." Goris sighed. "Regardless," she said, "we've got to do some further study before we start sending groups of colonizers out there. Something on three-oh-nine-bee has had a profound effect on our Explorer friends here, and potentially on us too. No matter whether we agree on that or not, we've got to find out what the substance is."

Marna spoke to Goris and Trillig silently inside their minds, "Nothing there was harmful to us, as far as we have been able to tell. So why don't we begin by exposing single compounds to other individual Explorers and see what happens?"

Goris looked at Trillig for confirmation that he had received the message. "Well, what do you think?" she said. "Shall we?"

***

The two science team leaders had no trouble convincing the powers that be to do further experiments with the little Explorers. Sarspec, along with the other members of the council, was eager to make sure that the new planet would sustain them for a few generations at least. "Do whatever you need to do to the little things and get us some results! My apartments are beginning to smell strange and my cough is getting worse. We need to move quickly!" he said. "Dissect them and examine all of their organs if you must. We need proof that it is safe to move on this. Now."

It was no surprise to the scientists that the members of the council treated the living Explorers as they treated all of the resources on Grendille. Trillig and Goris along with everyone else had been raised to think of their species as supreme to all around them, as though everything on Grendille, living or dead, was for their use, even if it meant fouling their own future. Goris felt sorely tempted to tell Sarspec that he needed to be more like Marna and Sparstie if they were going to have any chance for continued survival in the universe, but she somehow managed to keep quiet.

As they walked back to the lab and the waiting Explorers, Goris spoke quietly to Trillig. "I wanted to tell that old so-and-so just what he could do with his strange smells and his blasted cough!"

"Now, now, Goris," said Trillig patting his colleague on the arm. "You did the right thing keeping quiet. But listen, if you *are* right, and it *is* something that the Explorers brought back with them that has made me more aware of the situation we all are in danger of repeating, then once we expose the council to the substance, they too will see the light and clean up their act. Three-oh-nine-bee will be in no danger of being turned into a waste dump like poor old Grendille!" Trillig was still unconvinced of Goris' theory, but he wanted badly to prove that three-oh-nine-bee was safe and that they could start evacuating the scientists soon. His calculations were showing that the worsening of the planet's atmosphere was happening at an accelerated rate. He didn't want to be stuck on this horrible little trash-heap of a planet when the filters and scrubbers could no longer keep up. Already they were beginning to fail. His step quickened with his feeling of urgency and Goris had to jog to keep up.

"Hey, wait up, you need me to open the curtain!" she said to her colleague's back.

***

After three days of working nearly around the clock, the two scientists were running out of potential candidates. They had exposed nearly every Explorer to nearly every sample brought back from three-oh-nine-bee and still had not managed to cause any of the Explorers to become telepathic or exhibit signs of becoming conscious. "Well," Trillig said, "no luck. None of this stuff has had any effect." He glanced over at Marna who was watching them intently while they worked and he lowered his voice, whispering in Goris' ear, "But at least we haven't killed any of them."

Marna tilted her head and spoke to him in her way. "Don't forget, Trillig. I not only send my messages into your mind, but I receive them that way as well." Her mate, Sparstie, nodded in agreement.

Sincere apologies to the two of you, Marna," said Goris, "I'm sure Trillig meant nothing by it. We are just working so hard. I am getting close to exhaustion." Goris looked at her long fingered hands curiously. They looked paler than their usual healthy grey. "If you will excuse me, I think I'm going to go lay down in the back for a while." Goris shuffled off, slowly rubbing her large black eyes, into the room adjacent to the main laboratory that housed several cages of Explorers.

Long ago, Goris, the dedicated biologist and single female, had put a small sleeping pod in the little room and often stayed there at night, allowing the quiet chirps and coos of the Explorers to send her to sleep. Exhausted, she entered the room and slid down into the sleeping pod. She felt terrible. So tired, but something else as well. The thoughts inside her mind were frightening, disturbing, and she fell at once into a dream state, where all the weight of Grendille was crushing her chest, flattening her like clay, before she dried into dust and blew away with a hot wind. Into nothingness.

***

In the lab, Marna was speaking to Trillig. "You are right," the Explorer said into his mind. "I sense that none of the other Explorers have 'become' like we have. You have tried nearly everything. Would you mind if I had direct contact with one of them?"

The other Explorers had been kept separate from Sparstie and Marna, just on the slight chance that they could cause some kind of contamination. "I really don't see what that would achieve. We've exposed them to almost all of the samples from the pouch as well as the samples that we took from you and Sparstie. I really don't see what else it could be." He shrugged his slender shoulders. " But, go ahead, I suppose it can't hurt."

Marna approached the scientist and leapt onto his shoulder as he opened the cage of the young female Explorer that he had been about to expose to yet another extract from a soil sample. The creature looked up lazily with her large round eyes as Marna leapt into the cage and began to nuzzle the youngster and stroke her fur. "It's alright," Marna spoke telepathically to the creature. "It's okay. Do you have a name?"

Marna looked up at Trillig and blinked. "I don't know what I expected, but I guess you are right. Poor dumb creature. Nameless to herself and destined to be a laboratory animal and mother of generations of laboratory animals just like her." She looked back to the young Explorer and once again stroked her fur. "If only you could tell me your name."

Suddenly, the young Explorer's eyes opened wide. Her face no longer looked sleepy and dull. The creature gazed at Marna with a look of apparent surprise and fascination. Tentatively she reached out with one long fingered hand and touched the elder Explorer, prompting Marna to send her another message; a repeat of the basic question, "Do you have a name?"

"Why, why," the little Explorer's thoughts stammered, "I, I am Yorille. Yes, that is who I am. Yorille." Sparstie hopped across the room then, leaping onto Trillig's shoulder to get a better view of the newly awakened member of his species. Marna looked back at them, scientist and Explorer, satisfaction showing on her tawny face, before she realized that the scientist had not been able to hear the response to the simple question.

"She says her name is Yorille!" She shook her head at the thought of what she perceived to be the scientist's failure. "I forgot, Trillig! You cannot hear a message that is not directed at you!"

"What? Really, she has, um, as you say, she 'became'?" said an excited Trillig.

The little creature looked at the human with surprise and delight as she found that she could understand his speech. "Yes," she said to him telepathically, "I am Yorille!" and she hopped out of the cage after the Explorer Marna.

Trillig watched as the Explorers hopped about on the desks, chairs, and tables, smiling at witnessing the delight of the newly awakened Yorille. "Hey, we've got to go wake up Goris!" he exclaimed. "This is truly amazing! There is something *on* you, or *in* you, Marna, that has done the trick." He spoke in a rush, theorizing about what might have happened. "Maybe there's something that needs a living host, or the warmth from your body!" he paused, putting his long grey fingers to his forehead. "We've still got a lot to discover! But now we can try to awaken the council members!" Trillig frowned as he rubbed his temples. He still thought it would be a miracle if this stuff, whatever this stuff was, had any effect on closed-minded people like Sarspec. What if Goris' plan backfired and instead of the council members becoming more environmentally conscious they were just horrified by the idea of going to a planet where they would have competition from other thinking creatures? Would the Explorers simply be seen as competition for space and resources? "Well, now there are even more questions to be answered! But first things first, we must waken Goris and tell her the news! She will be thrilled!"

5 The Beginning of the End

The discovery of Goris' dead body came as quite a shock to Trillig. He had called politely through the ether curtain that served as a door to the room she was napping in and when she didn't answer, he put his long index finger into the door's alert niche and it sounded, making a jarring buzz. He really hated to awaken the sleeping biologist. She had looked so terrifically exhausted before her nap, but this news was important; Goris would *definitely* want to know about the awakening of the young Explorer as soon as possible. Since this interior door of the lab did not require the same security as did the main door, the ether curtain opened for him when he again placed his long index finger into the niche.

Trillig entered and saw Goris laying in the little slumber pod, looking as though she was merely in a deep sleep. But when Trillig called her name the third time and she remained motionless, the scientist got a sick feeling in the pit of his stomach. Somehow he knew that when he reached out his hand to touch her, her lifeless flesh would be ice cold. He didn't really know much about her, even though their paths had crossed professionally for almost his entire career, but he felt devastated even before he was sure of the truth of the situation.

"What could have happened?" Trillig muttered as he turned away from the room and returned to the main lab through the still open ether curtain. The scientist looked at Marna, who appeared to still be conversing with the newly awakened Yorille, probably silently explaining how it was that they had "become." Trillig cleared his throat and stood there, his slim shoulders slumped downward. "Marna, I, ah," he sputtered, at a loss for words, "it's... it's Goris... she's dead!"

The little Explorers, all three of them, considered him for a moment with their large unblinking amber eyes before going back to the silently telepathic conversation that they were having amongst themselves. Trillig tensed, his long fingered hands balled up into fists at his side. "Didn't you hear me? Don't you understand?" He said urgently, "It's Goris, she's dead. I mean, I thought she was tired, but..."

Marna looked at him again, this time with half lowered lids. The look seemed to say "so what" and a message appeared in his mind. "Nothing to be done about her, then. We have to keep working to awaken all of the Explorers. We must get them all into the pouches. Send them all to three-oh-nine-bee. To start our colony."

In an instant, Trilling made a chilling realization. He saw at once what had happened to Goris. He suddenly knew that whatever it was that these creatures had brought back with them, whatever it was that had given them the ability to think and communicate, it wasn't going to awaken the people of Grendille to some splendid new dawn of caring about their environment. There wasn't going to be an idyllic colony where the people treated their new home planet with reverence. Whatever this stuff was, it was going to awaken all of the Explorers, that was certain. But it was also going to destroy everyone else. All of them. The council members, the farmers, the teachers, the children, the scientists, himself. This was to be the new dawn for the Explorers, and Sparstie and Marna knew it. Trillig felt it in his atoms. Somehow, Trillig knew that this would be the end of his own species' time and the beginning of the time of the Explorers. "We don't know that, Trillig. We don't know for sure what has caused Goris to die. It could easily have been anything," said Marna, reading his thoughts. "Regardless, we must continue with the work, continue with *our* work."

Book Three – Here and Now

1 Regroup

Trudy frowned at the telephone receiver. Of course, there was no answer. Her family had gone gallivanting off to Texas and had totally forgotten all about her. They didn't call, they didn't answer and most likely they had just let their phone batteries run out of juice. "Well," she thought, "At least I hope they haven't gotten themselves lost." Her husband's sense of direction used to be uncanny. He could find his way in and out of any wilderness area without ever consulting a map or compass. But since portable Global Positioning System devices had come along, Trudy worried that it was the crutch that would cause her family to wander aimlessly around the forests of Texas once their phone batteries ran down. "Oh, don't be silly," she said to herself. "Why must you always worry?" She paused for a moment in her thoughts then answered her own question. "Because I'm a Mom. It's in the job description. Line one, paragraph one, I believe."

Trudy was anxious to find out if Frank and the kids had heard anything about that meteor that she had seen pass overhead. She read that it had likely landed somewhere in east Texas, but of course the chances were slim to none that it had ended up anywhere near where her family was looking for their Lingerling. Working on this advertising project for the space tourism company had given her a touch of outer space fever and she just wanted to talk to someone about meteors, or stars, or rocket ships to the moon. Actually, Trudy was feeling more than a bit lonely and just wanted to talk to someone about anything at all. "Ya know, I think I'll give the park rangers a call in the morning. Not that I'm checking up on them or anything. I just want to hear about that meteor..."

***

Wralis stirred where he lay in his weird green pod. Frank had placed the pod in the shade, resting it on a soft bed of burnt pine needles and leaves covered by an old sweatshirt of Philo's. The creature let out a small high pitched chirrup, the first sound they had heard either of the Explorers make, and looked more alert and decidedly more alive than he had when his limp body had been pulled from the wrecked space pouch. Dadive suddenly stopped relaying the history of the Explorers into Shawn and Marsha's minds and hopped over to her mate and looked intently at him. Wralis responded with a similar intent stare and it appeared as though the two of them were deep in thought-conversation.

As Marsha looked at the two of them her insides churned. When Wralis had interrupted the telling of their origin story by Dadive, Marsha was left hanging. She had so many questions. Had Wralis stopped Dadive from finishing the story on purpose? Marsha looked to her brother Shawn, who appeared calm and happy at the improved health of Wralis. Apparently the story didn't ring any alarm bells for him. Hadn't he received the same information as his sister? Or hadn't he arrived at the same dramatic conclusion? Marsha had a sick feeling from listening to Dadive's tale that whatever it was that caused these tarsier-like creatures to become thinking, communicating, supposedly sentient beings, whatever the bacteria or microbe or virus was, Marsha couldn't help but conclude that it had been deadly to the people of Grendille. The scientist had died, just as the Explorers "became", but why? Marsha could hardly stand the thought that whatever it was that caused the death of Goris, that it could have killed everyone on Grendille and it could possibly be lethal to the people of Earth too!

Dadive looked at Marsha and gave no indication that she had been eavesdropping on Marsha's suspicious thoughts. But even if Dadive had been listening in, Marsha felt that it probably wouldn't matter to her anyway. Marsha still felt a coldness about the creature that belied her adorable appearance. As far as Marsha could tell, Dadive was all business, all the time. She was an Explorer on a mission and her next thought-message expressed her urgency. "Wralis is improving, but he wishes to rest for a while longer. It is imperative that we look for the other pouch. I propose that Shawn and I go looking. He and the one you call Frank say they saw one of the Explorers, did they not? They must show me where."

Shawn looked to his dad and said, "We *think* we saw one, right, Dad?" Shawn laughed and said, "Oh, sorry Dad, I keep forgetting you can't hear her. Dadive wants to let Wralis rest a bit longer, but she's asking us to go with her and look for the other Explorers. Do you think you can remember where we saw that other one?"

Frank scratched the stubble on his chin. They had been out in this forest for two nights and another night was nearly upon them. They were in need of replenishing their food and water and it would be great to get back to the truck and charge the phone and make sure the rangers were informed that they'd be out here a while longer. Of course, he should inform Trudy, too. She might be worried about their silence. "Sure, well, at least I know it was in between here and there," he chuckled, and then felt stupid, remembering how daft his thoughts had been when he was under the effects of the Explorers' locator beacon. He cleared his throat and presented a plan. "Actually, I think it's a good idea. We'll leave our gear with Philo and Marsha, so that they can look after Wralis, and you and I will take a couple of empty packs back to the truck and refill them with supplies, food and water, and we'll charge the phones too. Then we can search for the other pouch in the morning. The setting sun will show us the way. Sound like a plan?"

Marsha nodded. "Do you think you guys can make it to the trailhead before dark?" she asked.

"Yeah, I think we can make it before then, it shouldn't be more than a couple of miles. We'll stay the night at the truck and be back sometime tomorrow about midday. If we don't find the other pouch in the morning, we can replenish Marsha and Philo's supplies, give them a charged phone and head out again." Frank was so focused on figuring out how to find the truck again that he really didn't care about looking for the pouch in the morning. He was trying to stay positive about not staying lost and about the weird turn that their fun little expedition had taken.

Dadive wasn't happy about the delay caused by the trip back to the truck, but when it was explained to her that the humans couldn't survive on worms and water drops, she had to agree to the proposal. The three of them set off right away, with Frank and Shawn doing the walking and Dadive hitching a ride on Shawn's shoulder.

The Lingerlings

***

When the trio was out of sight, Marsha breathed a sigh of relief. She wanted to talk to someone without Dadive listening in. Marsha had been alarmed by the Explorer's story, and she wanted to tell Philo the last part of the story about the scientist's death and see if he shared her concerns. Marsha wondered if Wralis could hear her thoughts, but it seemed as though he was still pretty absorbed with the task of healing, so she felt fairly confident that if she took Philo some distance away she would be able to speak freely. She wasn't sure even why she wanted to hide her concerns about the Explorers from Wralis. She hoped that she was using some poor logic with regards to the story that Dadive had been telling her and had jumped to a flawed conclusion about what had become of the people of Grendille. Perhaps she was wrong. Maybe they all lived happily together on the planet three-oh-nine-bee, the Explorers and the people. Marsha hoped most of all that the Explorers intentions here on Earth were not malicious ones.

***

The small space explorer stroked the vial that hung around her neck with her long index finger. "Our mission is in danger of failing," she told her colleague and companion. "I believe the pouch will repair itself, but not in time to rendezvous with the ship. They should have sent another pouch by now. We should have made contact. Either with the rescue pouch or the ancient ones. Something is wrong." Toriol continued stroking the vial. "At least the serum is safe."

Berndor blinked, his large eyes shining. "Success is still within our reach then. Our kind will not die out. We will find the ancient ones. We will help them 'become'. This new planet will be ours."

2 Trailhead

Shawn and his father reached the trail that would take them back to their truck even sooner than they expected. It seemed that the place where Wralis and Dadive's pouch had crash landed wasn't terribly far off the main trail after all. They had oriented their path just to the north of the lowering sun and ran into the trail marked with cairns not three miles away. Frank breathed a sigh of relief at finding the trail. In spite of what he had told Marsha about how near he thought it was, he had been somewhat worried that he was wrong and that they could be miles off into the woods and totally lost. The fear had been nagging at him for a while, but now that the little matter of being lost was off his mind, he was free to think about other things. Frank's thoughts eagerly returned to that Lingerling that he and the kids had originally come to Texas in search of.

Frank looked at the Explorer perched on Shawn's shoulder and addressed it. "Um, Dadive?" he said uncertainly. "Shawn, can she hear me?" The little Explorer looked at Frank and blinked her large round eyes slowly.

"Sure, she's listening, Dad. What do you want to tell her?" asked Shawn.

"Well, it's about the Lingerling. You know, the creature that we came out in search of. The omomyid. I'm wondering, how long ago did the first pouch land? I mean, the one that we are looking for..." Even though Frank knew from Shawn and Marsha that Dadive was an intelligent alien, he still felt silly talking to a tarsier about space ships. He swallowed hard and continued. "I'm thinking that what the hunter saw was one of the Explorers from the other pouch that you said landed somewhere around here. I think that Mr. Shepherd didn't really see an omomyid. I mean, it's a little crazy, but I'm thinking that the original Explorers, the ones that you guys are here looking for, the ones that got sent out in pouches from Grendille in hopes of finding another planet to colonize, I think that those Explorers may have actually been the omomyids that we find fossilized remains of here in Texas. They might have been the origin; the Adam and Eve if you will." There was no change in expression on the little Explorers face. Frank got no clue from her whether or not this made any sense or even whether or not she was actually listening.

Shawn said, "She's still listening Dad, but she doesn't understand what you mean by fossilized remains. She says the other pouch landed a while ago, but I don't know what she means by 'a while'. She says the Explorers in the first pouch were supposed to find their ancestors and 'awaken' them somehow, but that contact was lost and so that's why she and Wralis are here. She says that the first pouch was carrying something important."

Frank stroked the stubble on his chin. He was still looking forward to shaving it off, but it was a nice thing to stroke while thinking. "Dadive, what I guess I'm wondering is, how long ago did those original pouches leave Grendille in search of a new planet? Are we talking months, or years, or centuries, or what?"

Shawn looked into the face of the creature on his shoulder as she transmitted a message into his mind. He furrowed his brow as he struggled to understand what Dadive was telling him. "Dad," he said, "I think their time and our time are kind of skewed. I'm not sure I know how to translate what she's telling me. I'm kind of guessing that the Explorers live a really long time. At least they do since they had the awakening. After they 'became,' time changed for them if that makes any sense. It feels like what she's saying is that the original Explorers, the ones that didn't come back when they were sent on their mass reconnaissance by the people of Grendille, um, she says that they *could* have been sent here millions of our Earth years ago. But the one that the hunter saw, that one most likely came in the other pouch much more recently to search for the original ones.

138

Maybe just in the last month. So, maybe you're right, Dad. Maybe Dadive and Wralis have come to Earth hoping to find the omomyids that disappeared from Texas millions of years ago!"

Frank's eyes opened wide in pleasant surprise. "Ya know, I need to charge up this smart phone and get on the internet. This sounds to me as though there aren't any Lingerlings at all, but maybe something far more fantastic. Maybe I'm adding two and two and getting five, but aren't we descended from primates? Or at least we share a common ancestor. Sounds crazy, but I think it may be that Dadive and her kind could be our missing link to the stars!" said Frank, half laughing.

"Oh, c'mon Dad, I heard myself say that these guys might have visited Earth millions of years ago, but you're not saying, I mean, you don't think we are descended from them, do you? You don't think that human beings are the great great great grand children of alien tarsiers from another planet, do you?" said Shawn, happily aghast at his own suggestion.

"I dunno boy, I'm not even totally certain that modern tarsiers are all that closely related to the omomyid. Maybe they're more like great great great great cousins twice removed or something. But, well, what if one of the earliest primates on Earth was actually a pair of Explorers from the planet Grendille that landed here in east Texas? Wouldn't that mean that humans were in some small way related to aliens?"

***

Frank, Shawn and the little Explorer Dadive were silent as they walked, with all three of them thinking about the omomyids and the Lingerlings and the Explorers and what it could all mean. Shawn was speechless after what his father had said; he found it both thrilling and disappointing to think that humans might actually be related to aliens. Frank wondered what, if anything, this could mean about the biology shared throughout the Universe. But for Dadive, the concept of finding out that her ancestors might be extinct merely meant a wasted journey and a failed mission. With each of them deep in thought, it wasn't long before the wooden bulletin board and the parking lot beyond it came into view. "Okay," said Frank "looks just like we left it, except for that other truck. I wonder if the park ranger has been by to check on our permit."

"We haven't been gone all that long, Dad. It just feels like it because of all that brain fuzz that we had to shake off. Once Dadive turned off the beacon, time and space returned to normal!" said Shawn, adding, "Well, not normal exactly, but you know what I mean..." Shawn slung off his nearly empty pack as they reached the truck. " Jeez, Dad, that reminds me, what're we going to do about our little space traveler friend? I mean we can't go telling the park ranger about Dadive can we? Not until we really know what's going on. I mean, you know how the government would swoop down on the place! There'd be Air Force special UFO units and scientists and generals and everything; just like in E.T.!"

140

Frank gave his son's observation some consideration, again stroking his stubble. "Well, I don't know about the government swooping down with UFO experts, but I'm pretty sure an ambulance would swoop down and pack us all off to some sort mental health facility if we started telling everyone about giant nuts from space landing in east Texas. No, you're right. We've got to be very careful what we say to anyone. If the park ranger comes by, we should hide your little friend there."

"What about Mom? Does that include not telling Mom?" asked Shawn.

"Ooh, I'd hate to lie to your mom. You know how she is about lies of omission... Well, we'll have time to think about what to say to her while the phones recharge..."

***

"Philo, I really need to talk to you in private," whispered Marsha, drawing her cousin away by the arm. The two of them were standing some distance away from where the little Explorer lay in his pod. "I think Wralis is asleep; I don't want him to hear what I'm about to say."

Philo gave his cousin a funny look but followed her off into a more wooded area. "Whaddya mean you don't want Wralis to hear? What are you trying to hide? I know it's probably unnerving to have someone read your mind, but they seem harmless enough. So cute with those big eyes!" He wiggled his fingers over his eyes as though batting long lashes.

141

Marsha smiled in spite of her dark thoughts. "Yeah, they're cute alright, I'm just hoping they aren't deadly too!"

Philo guffawed. "Are you kidding me? You think they went from being lab rats to being ruthless killers? What in the world are you basing this hypothesis on?"

Marsha held her finger to her lips in an effort to get Philo to be quiet. "Well," she began, taking a deep breath and glancing around the pine tree to make sure Wralis hadn't stirred. "I'm not sure I'd use the term *ruthless*. Maybe *accidental* killers would be more precise. You remember what I was translating to you from the story that Dadive was telling us? About how the Explorers had been sent from the planet Grendille to find a new planet to colonize and how some came back from one such place, planet three-oh-nine-bee, with the ability to think complex thoughts and also to communicate telepathically?" Philo nodded and made a circular "come on" motion with his hand hoping Marsha would get to the point. "Okay, well, when we were interrupted, when Wralis woke up and told her to go and look for the others, well, she was just about to tell us something important. I know it. She was going to tell us something important *and* awful about what happened to the people that lived on Grendille. I got the feeling that Wralis intentionally stopped her from telling us."

"What what makes you think that? Did she say that the people, the aliens or humanoids or whatever they are, aren't still

142

around? Did Dadive say that they didn't all go to three-oh-nine-bee and start this new colony?"

"Well, no, she didn't, I mean, she didn't get to finish the story, don't you see? But I didn't get to translate to you the last part of what she was saying either. She had just been talking about how the first pair of Explorers to 'become' were teaming up with the scientists to find out what had caused them to awaken, become... whatever."

"Yeah, I got that much. You said that the Explorer Marna was working with the biologist Goris and some other guy; I forget his name, and then what?"

"Trillig, the other guy was named Trillig. He and Marna had just 'awoken' another of the Explorers, one who hadn't ever gone to any other planets; some young Explorer who only lived in the lab... But when Trillig went to tell Goris the exciting news, he found her dead. Ya know, dead. Lifeless, expired, kicked the bucket, not alive. And that's when Wralis interrupted."

Philo frowned, trying to see what this could mean. Obviously Marsha thought it was significant. He put his hand to his forehead and closed his eyes in an effort to concentrate his thoughts. "Okay," he said, trying to clarify what was fact and what was conjecture, "The Explorers came to Earth; two pouches of them, hoping to find Lingerlings, of that we are pretty much sure. Probably the ancient Explorers they are looking for were left here accidentally when they were searching for a new home planet to replace Grendille." He stopped talking again, opened his eyes and sighed. Suddenly Philo made a realization. "Maybe they've actually come looking for the omomyids that were here in Texas millions of years ago!" He looked up at Marsha and continued. "Do you think it's been that long since they abandoned Grendille?"

"Geez Philo, I don't know about that!" Marsha said in a hurried whisper. "What I'm talking about is what happened to the people? The people of Grendille? What happened to Goris? Did whatever happened to the biologist happen to *all* of the people? Did whatever killed her, kill all of them? And more importantly, could it happen to us?"

"Marsha, you're losing me. All I'm hearing from Dadive's story is a tale about Explorers searching through the stars for their long lost ancestors. No mass murders."

"Well, yeah, we can keep going over exactly who it is the Explorers came looking for and how long they've been here or there, whatever, but what I gather is that Dadive and Wralis came to Earth to expose these ancestors to the same stuff that awakened them and gave them the powers of thought and communication. Do you see what I'm saying? Philo, I'm not searching for some conspiracy theory; I simply think that it's possible that the wonderful thing that made the Explorers 'become' may well be the horrible thing that made the people of Grendille 'be not'!"

144

3 Aliens

The next morning Shawn and Frank awoke to the sound of someone or some thing tap-tapping on the pickup truck's window. Instead of going to all the trouble of pitching a tent they had decided to just sleep in the cab of the truck. They had reclined the seats as far back into the extra space of the king-cab as they could go and put their sweatshirts across their shoulders against the slight evening chill. As Shawn's sleepy brain began to determine the source of the tapping, he could feel Dadive begin to stir underneath his gray hoodie and he sent her a silent message telling her to stay put. Frank blinked and rubbed his face, still badly in need of a shave, and rolled down his window.

"Howdy, folks, sorry to wake ya. Where's the rest of the group? Didja find that critter y'all was lookin' fer?" drawled the park ranger with a friendly grin.

"Mornin'," said Frank amiably in return. "We left my daughter and her cousin out on the trail. Shawn and I wanted to come back and get some supplies, recharge our phones and make sure the wife wasn't worried." He purposely didn't answer the question about the critter, preferring avoidance to outright lying.

The ranger shifted his weight from his left to his right foot and pushed his hair off of his forehead with the back of his hand. "Yeah, actually, we got a call from your wife early this morning. Trudy, is it? Seems she was sort of concerned since she didn't hear from you. I told her we've all been having trouble with our cell phones around here lately, maybe on account of the meteor that flew on through. Well, at least that's what we wanna blame it on. Your wife was really interested in the meteor. Says she saw it all the way in New Mexico. How about that! She wanted to know if anybody knew where it landed, but I told her no such luck. Not unless you guys seen it?" The ranger laughed lightly and ran the toe of his work boot through the gravel of the parking lot. "Anyway, I promised I'd check on you and looks like y'all is just fine."

"Hey, thanks for doin' that; I 'preciate it. I'll be giving her a call as soon as I wake up a bit." Frank reached for the pink slip of paper on the dash. "Do we need to get another permit?"

"Nah," came the reply, "just leave a note sayin' how much longer you plan on bein' out there, okay?" The ranger strolled over to the other pickup now parked in the small dirt lot and

146

peered through the windshield and frowned. Then he waved goodbye without looking, and called back over his shoulder, "Y'all have a good day, hope you find that critter yer lookin' fer!" Then he climbed back on the little green four wheeler and drove away.

Dadive poked her head out from under Shawn's sweatshirt and watched with a placid expression as the park ranger drove away. Shawn sensed that she was only mildly curious about the humans, and so he silently asked the little Explorer how he and his kind compared to the people back home. Her reply drifted into his mind like the memory of a lesson learned in school. Dadive showed him mental pictures; still images like illustrations from a history text book that flowed directly onto imaginary screens behind his eyes. Shawn witnessed a virtual slide show of creatures that looked like something kind of familiar, a cross between the humans of Earth and the aliens of so many visitation myths and matinee movies, but the images really reminded Shawn of educational posters he had seen in pre-school. Like those funny old posters that were intended to show families, or occupations, or teach hygiene skills, the images included groups of humanoids involved in various, supposedly ordinary, activities. It was just that the people in the pictures were way out of the ordinary.

The people were of strange complexion, with enormous black eyes and thin lipped narrow mouths. Their features were smooth and subtle, having almost no noses or ears to speak of and their faces almost appeared to melt down into their long necks. Their entire bodies were long in all respects; their proportions were elongated. They were taller, thinner, and with sparser hair than humans and their hands resembled that of the Explorers with very long fingers, one of which was even longer than all the rest. Perhaps the most remarkable feature was that their skin appeared to come in a various cool hues of bluish to greenish grey. They were shown wearing an unusual manner of clothing, and Shawn's lack of familiarity with the creatures made it difficult for him to discern if they were men or women, because they appeared to Shawn to have no gender differences.

Shawn was mesmerized as the images melted together in his mind's eye, one flowing into another. Pictures of people going about their daily business. Adults, children, babies. Technicians, shopkeepers, teachers. Working, eating, playing. The pictures of interior spaces, the living rooms and sleeping chambers, and of the exterior spaces, the architecture and cityscapes, were remarkably like here on Earth, in that they seemed to be constructed or arranged for similar earthly functions, but the colors were odd and the shapes unfamiliar.

Shawn could tell that some of the images were of exterior spaces because they showed buildings and vehicles, and they reminded Shawn of a trip he had taken with his family to Manhattan when he was small. Shawn's six year old self had been surprised at how much it was like being indoors even when you were in a park with all those tall buildings around, but in these images, there was no feeling of nature at all. It was though outside and inside were the same thing. In fact, in every seemingly exterior image the sky appeared to be a façade, just some strange gauzy substance projected with lights, colors and shapes. Indeed it gave Shawn the feeling that everywhere was either indoors or underground and that all of the things in the images, other than the people, were manufactured as opposed to being naturally occurring.

When the images began to fade Shawn shook his head and blinked hard trying to retain the pictures for as long as he could. Finally though, the telepathic slide show ended, and Shawn grinned and exclaimed aloud, "Wow. Wow! Is that what it's like where you're from?"

"No," Dadive replied silently, "that is what we have been told used to be. You asked what the people were like. This is what I know, but there are people no more. I have shown you images from the past, from history. These pictures were from Grendille. Long ago, before the Second Exodus."

Frank looked over at Shawn who looked blown away by whatever it was that Dadive had been telling him about. "This certainly is frustrating only hearing half of the conversation," Frank said. "And I have a feeling I keep hearing the less interesting half, too!"

Shawn looked at his Dad and stammered, "I, uh, she, uh, Dadive has been showing me pictures of life on Grendille. From before they all left. Pictures, Dad, into my head, it's extraordinary! Pictures of buildings, rooms, people. I am one of the first humans to really see alien life! Real alien life forms!"

Dadive considered Shawn for a moment before replying, "To me, of course, *you* are alien life. But the images? That life that I have shown you? Call them the people if you like, but they exist no more. If you, Shawn, have encountered alien life, it is only Wralis and I that you have seen. We are the aliens here. Our kind and the other lower life forms on our planet are all that we know of. In fact, other than here on your planet, our home contains the only life we have encountered. And we Explorers have been to many places. Many planets."

"Of course," said Shawn, I didn't mean... I didn't mean that you and Wralis aren't aliens. I meant, aliens like, um, us. Like people. It's just that you seem so familiar to me. Your fur, your face, your arms and legs and tail. Like something from Earth. Like a regular tarsier. Like something I've seen at the zoo." Shawn thought for a moment. "Other than the telepathy, I mean." He had wanted to add that those other aliens were like real ones, like the ones you could buy from the gift shops in Roswell, but he didn't. Doubtless the little Explorer knew that's what he was thinking anyway.

Dadive closed her eyes and an uneasy feeling of that cold shutter being brought down again came to Shawn's mind. He suddenly felt icy and strange, and like he had managed to deeply insult Dadive and every Explorer that had ever been. Shawn wondered, did Dadive look down upon him and his family? She did not seem to hold the people that used to share the planet Grendille with the Explorers in very high esteem. Did Dadive view Explorers as better than people? And did she think of people, the humans of Earth and those extinct people of Grendille, as less than animals? Shawn supposed that she might have good reason to feel that way, after all, her ancestors were treated no better than lab rats, and according to Dadive, the people of Grendille had managed to destroy at least one planet with their waste and greed. Perhaps they had even managed to destroy themselves. "But it's not my fault; don't take it out on me," Shawn muttered under his breath.

***

Trudy jumped at the unexpected sound of the ringing of the phone. The house had been so eerily quiet lately that the phone cut through the quiet with all the surprise of a popped party balloon. "Oh gosh!" she said to Candy. "I sure hope it's Frank and the kids." She grasped the receiver before it could ring again. "Frank?" she asked hopefully.

"Hey, how did you know it would be me?"

"Oh, I was just hoping! How're things in Texas? You are still in Texas aren't you?" she asked.

"Frank smiled and said pleasantly, "Well, we did think we might have taken an accidental trip into The Twilight Zone there for a while! Look, Trudy, you won't believe all we've been experiencing!"

"You mean there's more to Texas than giant doughnuts? Don't tell me you found Bigfoot! Or more of those nasty chupacabras!"

"Hey, don't be flippant, I know you were worried. We just spoke with the park ranger and he told us you called." Frank squinted into the morning sun and continued. "Shawn and I came back to the truck to get some supplies and then we're going back out there."

Trudy was only half joking when she replied. "You mean you left my Marsha and Philo alone out there? You remember the last time the kids went camping without a grown-up! Mutant goats and chupacabras for real! You better be looking after those kids."

Suddenly Frank had an idea of how he was going to avoid lying to his wife and still keep her from getting worried. He would simply tell the truth. "Oh, don't worry Trudy, I'm looking after them! We had to leave them out there to look after Wralis. He's this little alien guy and he's recovering from a crash landing. I mean, somebody had to stay with him."

Trudy snorted a derisive laugh into the receiver. "Oh, right, I guess that shooting star wasn't a meteor after all but was actually an alien space ship entering the atmosphere? And you guys have managed to find the thing and naturally you're rescuing the occupants. You are such good Samaritans!"

"That's right, my dear; how'd you know? And now we're going back to help them with their mission. Dadive, she's the other alien, she's trying to find this other space ship that landed in the area not long ago and most likely has a damaged locator system or something," said Frank, trying hard to put a fake grin in his voice.

"Terrific, Frank, you guys have your fun, let me know if anything *really* happens and I'll see you when you get back. Remember, you've got a grown-up job waiting for you in Albuquerque; you can't be tromping around those woods forever!" Trudy shook her head and sighed, she had lived with this guy long enough to know when he was pulling her leg. He wasn't usually this blatant though. "Frank, you must think I'm getting old and daffy if you thought I'd fall for this story. Alien space craft indeed!" She laughed lightly, a lovely sound to Frank's ear. "Okay, go play, but if you really did leave Marsha and Philo alone in the woods, I want you and Shawn to get back with them ASAP. Okay? Alright, talk soon, love to the kids! Bye."

"Alright, Trudy, bye for now. Don't forget, I did tell you we found aliens, okay? You won't forget I told you?"

"No, Frank, I certainly won't forget, just let me know in advance if I need to make up the guest bed or set an extra place at the table before you bring them home." Trudy pressed the red "end" button and put the phone back in the charging cradle. "Silly man," she thought, "dear, dear, silly man."

"You're so smart, Dad!" said Shawn admiringly. "I'm a witness. You did tell her."

"Yup, I sure did!" he said grinning broadly. Then, with an attitude of triumph, Frank pulled his disposable razor from his bag and held it aloft as though he were King Arthur pulling the sword from the stone. And now, at last, to shave!"

4   The Search

Philo had a hard time falling asleep that evening. His mind raced off and on all through the night, yet he awoke early with the rising sun glaring right in his eyes. He'd been careful to pitch the tent well away from the still mending Explorer for fear that Wralis could hear his churning thoughts, but he hadn't really paid any attention to where the sun would be coming up to greet his closed lids. Looking out of the little screened window at his chosen sleeping spot he thought with amusement, "Yeah, I am so sure that this pine tree will shield me from any telepathic alien beings that are trying to get access to my thoughts."

It was the seed that Marsha had planted in his mind the night before that had left him so sleepless. Her words had given rise to questions about the intentions of these cute little critters from outer space. He had a hard time believing that they meant to harm anyone, but what if these aliens were bringing something with them that was deadly? From what Marsha concluded, the people of Grendille didn't survive contact with the substance that made the Explorers "become." Had they brought any of this substance with them to Texas? What if earthlings couldn't survive it either? It was alarming to think that the human population of the Earth might be in jeopardy from these big-eyed bush babies. Philo remembered seeing stuffed animals at the zoo gift shop in Albuquerque that looked almost exactly like the Explorers except that they came in pastel colors of pink and blue and made little giggling noises when you squeezed their tummies. Philo was trying hard not to let his thoughts run away with him; trying hard not to think that there was something sinister about these tawny visitors from another planet. They were just here looking for their ancestors. But why?

Philo turned onto his stomach in his sleeping bag and leaned on one elbow as he reached out to unzip the tent flap and greet the day. There, placidly looking back at him sat the little Explorer Wralis, apparently fit and healthy. Philo was startled and more than a little bit alarmed at the sight of him. Had he been listening in to Philo's thoughts? "Oh, um, good morning, Wralis. It looks like you are feeling better. I don't know if you can understand me," said Philo, somewhat flustered. "Um, ah, the others, I mean, Shawn and Frank and Dadive have gone off in search of the pouch. The other pouch, I mean, the one that landed around here earlier. Shawn and Frank thought they saw another Explorer a couple of days ago, and so they've gone off to look. They should be back to see how you are and drop off some supplies." Philo considered the creature who still sat staring with soft wide eyes back at him. "Um, are you hungry? Thirsty?"

Wralis tilted his head to the side and opened his eyes even wider. Philo took this as a sign of affirmation and so he got up and poured a small cup of water and set it down before the furry mammal. The Explorer picked up the cup in his two hands inserting his long index fingers over the rim and into the water. Then he tilted his head back and drank deeply of the water in a very human-like fashion. When he set down the empty cup, his expression changed slightly to one that appeared only somewhat satisfied.

"More?" asked Philo, wondering why he was speaking to the space traveler in single word sentences as though speaking to an infant. Philo found the cuteness of the creature to be disturbingly contradictory in light of the thoughts he had just been pondering. Looking up, Philo noticed Marsha watching from behind a tree some distance away. "Good morning, Cuz," he called, happy to see her friendly face and break his uneasy feeling.

Marsha walked over casually, lightly stepping over a couple of scorched pine cones. "Hey Philo; hey Wralis. Um, maybe you're wondering what's going on," she said, addressing the Explorer. "I don't know how much you remember, or what Dadive told you, but you've been recovering from a crash landing. You almost died. Dadive should be back soon." Marsha looked into the furry face of Wralis. He gave no sign that he understood her. If she didn't know any better, she would not believe that this creature was anything more than a typical tarsier, not that she was really all that familiar with tarsiers, typical or otherwise. The animal remained just as he was, sitting on his haunches and gazing dumbly at her, and it gave Marsha a creepy unsettled feeling and her stomach did a small flip.

"I say we pack up this camp, now that Wralis is better, and be ready to go and help look for the other pouch as soon as they all get back," said Philo, trying to put a light and airy tone to his voice.

Marsha began to look more and more rattled and finally she spoke, hoping to redirect her concern. "Yeah, sure, let's get ready to go look for this other pouch." She looked at the camping gear spread around, put her hands on her hips, and then she looked at Philo and frowned. "But then what? What are we going to do with *two* pouches of Explorers?" She began stuffing a sleeping bag into its sack. "What if the Lingerlings that they came in search of are the omomyids that became extinct millions of years ago and so their ancestors are just some fossils in the Museum of Natural Science in Houston?" Pulling the drawstring closed on the sack she continued talking, her tone becoming more highly pitched. "Or, what if their ancestors turn out to be the ordinary tarsiers that live in jungles almost half way around the world? What then?"

158

Philo looked at Wralis and the creature blinked. Even if the creature didn't understand him, Philo addressed him directly as though he did. "Wralis, we came out to Texas hoping to find living creatures that have somehow escaped being dead for thirty million years or more," Philo explained. "Some guy said he saw a living omomyid, and you guys sure do look like them." Philo paused and looked away from the creature to think about what he was saying and then he looked Wralis in the eyes and considered him for a moment. Again Wralis gave no indication that he was listening, but Philo continued. "What have you and Dadive come here looking for? Have you come here to find your ancestors and bring them back to your planet? Is that right? You want to take your ancestors back home?" Philo posed the questions as though he were asking a dog if it wanted a treat and he felt stupid for thinking that it would help Wralis to understand him.

Wralis continued sitting there with a blank stare on his face and Philo decided to ignore the creepy little presence and let his thoughts be known to his cousin. What difference could it make if the alien was or wasn't listening? "Marsha, I've been thinking about what you said. I mean, *all* night, thinking. I may be coming around to your theory." He glanced nervously at Wralis. "For some reason I thought that the Explorers wanted to find their ancestors and bring them home, but what if they really came here to colonize Earth? What if what they want is to find the original Explorers, the omomyids, the tarsiers, whatever, and help them to 'become' and then colonize our entire planet?" Philo looked again at the Explorer Wralis. "Look, Wralis, I don't know if you understand me, but Marsha and I are worried that you and Dadive have come to Earth with something that could endanger our planet. We fear that whatever the substance is that caused to Explorers to, ya know, 'become', that that substance was deadly to the people of Grendille and it could be deadly to us too."

"Finally!" said Marsha to her cousin, "That's what I've been trying to tell you! Now you see the problem!"

"Well, I see the *potential* problem," conceded Philo. "Marsha, we might be wrong. I hope we're wrong."

Philo and Marsha finished packing up all the camping gear, each wrapped up in his or her own thoughts, while Wralis watched. As Philo was squatting to stack the packed gear into one pile, Wralis approached him and looking directly into Philo's blue eyes, he blinked slowly. The creature then turned to look at Marsha and appeared to consider her for a moment before he tilted his head to the side and blinked slowly at her too. Then the creature reached out with one of his long fingers and began to draw in the dirt.

"What's he doing?" asked Philo. "Hey, I think he's drawing something. Yeah, Marsha, look. It looks like he's drawing a self portrait."

Wralis blinked up at them again, apparently making sure that they were looking, and then using the side of his hand, he erased the picture. Then turning away without a backward glance, he took off at a gallop into the woods.

***

Shawn and Frank had been walking for about a mile, both of them feeling refreshed from a nice breakfast of granola bars and juice and Frank was stroking his smooth stubble free chin. "It sure was nice to have bit of a wash!" said Frank happily. "A clean body and a clean mind! Helps now to be starting fresh on these weird thoughts I've been pondering. A new angle on things, right Shawn?"

"I sure hope so, 'cause you were coming up with some pretty wild and crazy theories last night. I mean, for a professional zoologist, it sure sounded like Dadive's beacon was still affecting your brainwaves!" Shawn smiled at the memory of how goofy they had all felt when they first arrived in this forest. It was a lucky thing that they didn't have anything serious happen, no broken bones or getting totally lost or anything, just a fuzzy-headed meander through the woods, something like Shakespeare's A Midsummer Night's Dream, but without the faeries.

"Well, okay, perhaps it did sound a little wild. Maybe I'm not totally up on every step on the evolution of man, I mean, I'm not sure of the exact place of primates like tarsiers and omomyids in the chain. I'm not sure if they're an offshoot, or on a main branch, or the trunk, but I'm just saying is this: what if the Explorers and the omomyids *are* one and the same? Wouldn't that make us related somehow?" asked Frank. "They appeared in Texas suddenly, and disappeared suddenly too. Maybe, just maybe, the omomyids came from Grendille and were successful here for a time…"

"Are you still saying that you think the Explorers are our distant cousins?" said Shawn, laughing. "Gee Dad, I guess I'm not ready to *be* an alien. I still want to collect the little plastic figures!"

During the time that the father and son were talking, Dadive was sitting on Shawn's shoulder looking about at the forest. Although outwardly she appeared placid, her annoyance was mounting. She was getting tired of waiting for the two to stop their conversation so that she could bring them back to the task at hand: looking for the other pouch. She concentrated on interrupting Shawn's thoughts, trying to turn them gently in her direction. "Shawn, remember what we are here for. We are looking for the Explorers. We need what they carry."

Shawn didn't notice that the thought was not his own. "Dad, we're supposed to be looking for the Explorers. Shouldn't we hustle back over to Philo and Marsha and give them some breakfast, check on Wralis, and then start looking?" he said, interrupting Frank's discussion of evolutionary theory.

"Wow, Shawn," exclaimed his father, "did you just say we should hustle? You must have had a good night's sleep. In spite of the cramped truck cab."

"Hey, it's better than the ground any day!" said Shawn with a grin, as he lightly leapt over a small tree branch that lay across the trail.

***

Shawn and his father were silent the rest of the way as they hiked straight back to where Philo and Marsha waited with the injured Wralis. Their intention was to drop off some supplies and then head straight out again to look for the other pouch, but when they got back to the scorched area, they were surprised to find no one waiting. No Philo, no Marsha, and no Wralis either.

"Hey, guys!" Frank called, "Philo! Mar-shaa!" Frank and Shawn walked around the crash site looking for perhaps a note or some sign that they had just gone for a little jaunt and would be right back. "Jeez, where could they have gone? They've packed up all the stuff, backpacks, both tents, water bottles, sleeping bags, everything. Maybe Wralis was feeling fine and they went to look for that pouch. But they can't communicate with Wralis without Dadive's help, can they? And why didn't they leave a note."

"Do you suppose they went off looking for us?" asked Shawn. "Maybe they went back to the parking lot and we somehow missed them."

"I dunno, maybe. But, um, does your little alien space friend have any clue? I mean, can Dadive talk to Wralis over distances? See if she can find out where Wralis is and if they're with him," said Frank, trying not to get upset at the thought of his daughter and nephew out missing in the woods.

Shawn looked into the face of the creature and spoke out loud. "How about it, Dadive, do you know where Wralis is? Is he with my sister and Philo?"

Dadive blinked in her usual slow way, making Frank feel more agitated and impatient. This was getting hard to take, Frank thought, and this alien tarsier, or whatever it was, constantly gave off a feeling of indifference as though its strange gift of telepathy and intelligence had eliminated any capacity for emotion or empathy. "They are not far. I sense that Wralis received a message, faint but definite, from the other Explorers."

"And Marsha and Philo followed him? Just took off?" said Shawn.

As usual, Frank was left out of the conversation. "What did she say? Where are they?"

"She said that Wralis heard the other Explorers calling, or something like that. She didn't say that Marsha and Philo went after him, but that's what they must have done."

"Can she lead us in the right direction? Maybe we should leave a note here, in case they come back," said Frank, fishing for a piece of paper and a pencil in his pack. "Jeez, for a couple of smart kids, they sure can be thoughtless! I'm disappointed that they didn't think to leave some kind of note for us!"

5 Mother?

Philo and Marsha were having some difficulty following Wralis through the east Texas forest, chasing the little creature and trying to keep an eye on him as he leapt from bush to tree to branch to bush to tree and so on. It wasn't easy following the sprightly Explorer, so recently on death's door, as he moved quickly and all but disappeared into the brush due to his tawny color. "So what was that picture he drew in the sand, Philo?" Marsha called to her cousin.

He replied over his shoulder, "Oh jeez, I dunno, looked like a picture of an Explorer! Then he wiped it away. I have no idea what he meant."

"We really should have left a note," said Marsha, winded from trying to talk while jogging to keep up with the creature.

"You saw how fast Wralis took off; there wasn't time for a note! It's getting really hard to follow him! Quickly, Marsha! He's getting ahead of us!"

The two of them were trying hard to keep up and Wralis was continuing to sprint ahead, giving them no indication of where he was going or if he knew they were trying to come too. He was making good use of any trees or bushes to keep himself off of the ground, leaping from branch to branch. Philo wondered what was the big hurry? Philo suspected that Wralis had received some sort of call from the other Explorers, the ones that originally came looking for their Lingerlings, but Philo wondered why Wralis hadn't waited for Dadive to come back with Frank and Shawn. He also wondered what message Wralis was trying to convey by drawing a picture of an Explorer and then erasing it. Suddenly, in a clearing just over a brush covered ridge, Philo saw the reason.

***

Shawn led the way with the little Explorer perched once again on his shoulder. They had left a note at the site telling Marsha and Philo in which direction they had gone, poking the paper onto a tree branch. A little higher up on the tree they had hung a small duffle bag containing some granola bars and juice boxes, just in case the two of them returned. Frank was almost certain that they hadn't just gone wandering off; at least Frank was trying hard to stifle his feeling that something might be wrong.

167

Luckily, Dadive was getting some sort of bearing on which direction Wralis had headed. She told Shawn that she wasn't totally certain, because the telepathic message that she was receiving was a bit confused. "I'm sensing," she told Shawn telepathically, "that something might be wrong with the Explorers that we were seeking. Not the ancestors, but our colleagues Berndor and Toriol."

Shawn had never heard Dadive refer to these other Explorers by name. He had assumed that Dadive didn't actually know them, but now he got the feeling that not only did she know them but she might even be related to them in some way. How Shawn got this feeling, he wasn't actually sure. Suddenly he addressed the creature out loud with a startling question: "One of them is your mother?!" but Dadive did not reply.

Frank and Shawn hurried off in the direction that Dadive had indicated. It was obvious to both of them that they were more worried about what had happened to the others, even the other Explorers, than Dadive was. She didn't appear to be worried about Wralis, or really even to be curious about him, aside from her desire to complete the mission. If it hadn't been her directive, Shawn thought that she couldn't have cared less where Wralis had gone and what had happened to him. Suddenly, something brightly colored up ahead and to the west attracted Shawn's attention and he got a shock of emotion. He veered toward the object, which turned out to be Marsha's water bottle, and as his finger tips touched the cool aluminum, he could immediately sense what his sister was seeing at that very moment. Shawn nearly fell over backward with the force of the feeling, the terror and sadness that he knew Marsha was experiencing at that very moment, and he shouted to his dad, "Danger, Dad, Marsha is in danger! They are all in danger! Hurry, this way!" and he ran off in the direction of his sister at a sprint, nearly knocking Dadive off his shoulder. The little Explorer gripped harder onto his shoulder, her long fingers gripping into the flesh beneath his tee shirt, as Shawn ran, crashing along through the underbrush.

Frank soon overtook his son, his longer legs and desire to protect his only daughter helping him to leap over the shrubs and brambles. "This way, Shawn, I know they're nearby!" Frank shouted, just as he got a glimpse of Marsha's pink t-shirt through the trees. "I hope she's okay, I hope she's okay," Frank silently chanted, glad that at least he was nearing where she was. "Marsha!" he shouted. "We're coming!"

Marsha turned at the sound of her father's voice and she shouted one word back to them. "Cougar!" she said, and turned away again.

***

The four humans stood around, looking down at the bloodied remains of the Explorer know as Toriol. "We couldn't help," said Marsha sadly. "We managed to chase the cougar away, but not before, well... you see." Marsha turned and walked a few paces away. She was still holding the stick that she had waved around to chase away the cat. Laying it down, she looked up, noticing the two Explorers, Dadive and Wralis, aimlessly walking around several yards away. Marsha could see through the trees that the area just beyond where they found themselves was burnt much like the crash site where they had only two days before discovered the Explorers and their strange space pouch. "Dadive!" she called to the Explorer. "Dadive, can anything be done?"

Dadive looked up at her and took a few bouncing steps closer. The creature glanced over at the bloody and torn figure lying on the ground without expression. "No," was the simple reply that came into Marsha's mind, as Dadive turned back away and went to join Wralis in their odd meandering. Marsha knew before she got the thought-message that it was hopeless. The injuries sustained by the Explorer known as Toriol were extensive. The cougar had ripped the tiny primate apart.

Philo shook his head as he looked down at the Explorer. He felt sad that a creature, especially one that had come from so far, had ended up as a potential meal for an east Texas wild cat. He looked up at Frank and said, "We were back at camp and Wralis seemed fully recovered. We gave him some water and tried to communicate with him, but it wasn't entirely successful. At first it seemed like he wasn't listening to us at all. Then he tried to communicate. He drew a picture in the sand. I think he drew this creature, Toriol. Then he erased the picture; brushed it away with his hand. I think he was trying to tell us she was in danger." Philo shifted his weight from one foot to the other and

170

pulled a small twig from his light colored hair. "Marsha and I were just finishing packing up the stuff, getting ready for when you guys came back for us, and Wralis just bolted. We didn't have time to think, so we just took off after him."

Marsha glanced again at the body of the Explorer. "Yeah, Wralis took off so fast, especially considering he'd been all but dead just a little while ago... I couldn't get any clear message from him and I don't know... it was probably just from how fast he moved that it seemed pretty clear that something was wrong." She looked toward Dadive and Wralis and gestured with her thumb. "You'd never know now that he was worried about his colleague. When we got here and saw the mountain lion tearing into Toriol, it was like Wralis was looking for something else. Maybe the other Explorer that's supposed to be with her? ...Or him? ...I dunno, which is it?"

Shawn spoke up. "Her. It's a her. Actually it's Dadive's mother."

Marsha looked shocked. "Are you sure? Her mother?!" As Shawn nodded, Marsha felt as though her suspicions about the little Explorers had been entirely confirmed. These creatures, cute though they may be, plus intelligent and telepathic, were nonetheless without emotion. They had intellectual intelligence, but no emotional intelligence. Dadive hadn't been concerned about Wralis when he was injured, knowing that he would self repair. But here she was, not concerned about her own mother, even though Dadive herself had said that no repair was

171

possible. How could a species survive like that? Mammals at many intellectual levels had emotional ties. Marsha had seen it for herself in dogs and cats and other pets that had passed through her life. Cats and dogs weren't as smart as these creatures, not by any stretch, but they had friendships and affections. How was it possible that the Explorers did not?

6 Searching

Frank and the others were timid about burying what remained of the Explorer, Toriol. They had witnessed the seemingly miraculous recovery of Wralis; they had seen his broken lifeless body that now appeared to be supremely lively and undeniably healthy, but Dadive assured them that there would be no such recovery for her mother. The cougar had taken the life of the little Explorer and she must be buried, an alien being put to rest in alien earth. Philo and Shawn walked about the area, looking for a suitable rock to place over the burial spot so that she would not be easily dug up by any scavengers, and also to mark the spot so that they would be able to exhume her body should they want or need to.

The teenaged cousins walked into the burnt clearing and saw the large nut-like space-pouch half buried in the ground just as Dadive and Wralis's had been. This pouch however, appeared to them to be in better condition; perhaps it hadn't suffered as much damage or perhaps it had already repaired itself in preparation for the return voyage. Philo looked around for Dadive, hoping to ask the Explorer about the passengers this pouch had held. Dadive and Wralis were nearby, still wandering about the area, and it appeared to Philo that they were looking for something, scanning the ground.

"Um, ah, Dadive? Was there a companion in this pouch? I mean, the pouch you came in carried the two of you. Didn't this pouch carry two Explorers as well?" Philo asked.

"Indeed," came the reply into Shawn's mind. Shawn turned to Philo and translated the telepathic message, "Yeah, she says."

"So where is that other Explorer? I mean, they seem to be searching for some*thing*; it sure doesn't look like they are searching for some*one*," noted Philo.

"You're right, Cuz," said Shawn, absentmindedly digging the toe of his hiking boot into the burnt ash surrounding the space pouch. "There was another Explorer. Dadive told me this other one was named Berndor." Shawn turned to look at Dadive. "What about it, Dadive?" he called over to her. "Why aren't you looking for the other Explorer? I mean, you're not, are you?"

Dadive spoke again into Shawn's mind. To Shawn, she sounded like she was getting tired of answering so many questions from the Earth humans. "No, we are looking for something far more important. Something that Toriol was carrying. Something that is very vital to our mission."

"Well, mighten it be, I dunno, just suppose, that this other guy, Bernie, has the thing? Or that maybe your mom stashed it in the pouch," said Shawn to Dadive.

Dadive did not look up at Shawn, but Shawn felt from her an exasperated sigh. The same kind of exasperated sigh that grown-ups sometimes direct at children when they lose their patience, when they are tired of answering silly questions. "No," Dadive at last replied, "Toriol would have had this thing on her."

Shawn tried to make light, hoping to banish some of the discomfort that Dadive was causing in him. He was getting to the point where he didn't much care if he irritated her, because he himself was being irritated by her cold and superior attitude. "What," he said aloud, jokingly, "something she had in her pockets?" He chuckled easily and the telepathic feeling that Shawn got from the Explorer in response was an almost physical sense of pain. Apparently Dadive didn't take kindly to Shawn's jokes. "Jeez, okay, just tell us what you're looking for; maybe we can help," he said, trying, but failing, to keep his own exasperation out of his voice. The message he got in return stated simply that "*they*" had helped enough. Then that same cold creepy feeling of a shutter closing down came into Shawn's mind.

***

Frank opened his pack and set out some lunch items on a sweatshirt that he had spread out on the ground. Although he wasn't receiving telepathic messages from the Explorers, he was getting a feeling of unrest and ill will from the creatures. Frank searched his mind while opening a canister of peanuts, trying to determine what it was that he was basing these unpleasant feelings on. He found it hard to put his finger on some concrete event or translated comment, and he couldn't really come up with anything aside from just a feeling of Dadive's generally cold attitude. Frank thought that maybe that was a telepathy of sorts. "On the other hand," Frank thought to himself, she is a scientist of sorts; a space traveler, an astronaut on a mission. Why should I expect her to behave as cute and cuddly as she looks? It makes more sense that the Explorers would be business–like. Right?" Frank continued as he set out the lunch stuff to ponder over the Explorers mission. Just how far had they had travelled to retrieve their colleagues? Were they just aiming for planet Earth in general? Or was there some specific plan to search for their ancestors in Texas? When he was finished setting out the crackers and dried fruit, he called to the three teens, who were some short distance away lounging in the shade, and once they had joined him, he voiced his thoughts.

"Kids, I've been thinking, about Dadive and Wralis. About them traveling through space in that little nut to find their colleagues, the other Explorers... Quite a tremendous accomplishment, don't you agree?" The three teens, nodded, mouths already full of fruit and granola bars as Frank shifted from his kneeling position to a sitting one. "Okay, but I'm feeling this coldness from them, and I'm trying to tell myself that they should be cold. They are astronauts on a mission after all, not three kids and a goofy biologist out on a camping trip. But still I can't shake this feeling that they are done with us. I mean, that they're sick of dealing with us." Frank paused, knitted his brows and wondered whether or not to continue. "I mean, I almost feel ashamed to say this, to sound so suspicious, but do you think they are malevolent? Do they mean harm?"

Marsha was the first to speak, glancing up to make sure that the Explorers were a good distance away. The little creatures could be seen, methodically still searching the ground, looking for something, on the far side of the charred clearing. "Listen, I've been feeling it too. Not that they are evil or anything, rather that they are emotionless, ya know? Certainly like they don't care for us, but also that they don't even care for each other!"

"Yeah," agreed Shawn, "and I've been feeling like Dadive's patience is wearing thin with us. I mean, with us humans. It seemed like she was initially happy to have our help and now she seems to be saying that she's done with us and we should get out of their way." Shawn looked perplexed and added, "But not in so many words. I just get the feeling that they don't have a very high opinion of people. Not us specifically, but when I asked Dadive about the people of Grendille she showed me still images. In my head, ya know. They were like pictures in a history book. Of a culture that had died. And, well, she seemed to be happy about that. Well, if not happy exactly, then satisfied.

Like she thought it was fitting that they were gone. Ya know, good riddance."

"So I was right," said Marsha, "the people are all gone…"

"So what do you think," asked Philo between bites, "should we do likewise? I mean, leave them here, go, get out of their way? It seems crazy to find a couple of aliens, say 'hi', say 'bye' and just leave 'em out here. But I don't know that we can help them. Or that they want us to."

Frank unscrewed the top of an aluminum water bottle and put it to his lips before replying, "You are certainly right there. I mean maybe she doesn't want us, but… I still want to know… I want to know, what exactly *is* their mission? Dadive came to find her mother, but what did her mother come for? What did she bring with her that is so important?" Frank screwed the top back on the bottle and set it on the ground beside him. He looked over at Dadive and her mate. "I'm pretty sure they came to find the omomyids, right? But what the heck are Wralis and Dadive searching for now?"

Shawn furrowed his brow as if deep in thought. "Dad," he said, "Remember when we were walking back to the parking lot? Remember Dadive was saying that they were here to 'awaken' their ancestors? Remember? Maybe I wasn't translating every word, but I'm sure that's what she said: that the first pouch came here to find and 'awaken' the Lingerlings. Do you think that the first pouch brought something along with them, some magic potion or something, that is supposed to cause Earth's tarsiers to "become" just like the Explorers? Is that what Dadive and Wralis are looking for? Is that what they are trying to do?"

7 The Vial

Frank and the three teenagers nibbled on their lunch and rested in the shade, each of them trying to figure out what the Explorers were up to, and what, if anything they could or should do about it. They watched as Dadive and Wralis continued to hunt for their certain something, heads down, occasionally moving aside a leaf or pinecone to peer underneath, and walking in ever widening circles. Eventually, their circles began to bring them nearer to where the humans sat, and Marsha worked hard at trying to formulate a question for Dadive that would elicit the greatest amount of information about the mission before Dadive could once again lower that creepy shutter that put an end to communication. It was difficult for Marsha to control her thought emotions, and so she worked at thinking cool, scientific thoughts, hoping to keep her feelings of concern and suspicion at bay. Finally Marsha perceived that Dadive was near enough to be receptive to her telepathically and so she silently asked, in as innocent a way as she possibly could, "What does it look like? What does this thing that you are looking for look like?"

Dadive did not look up from her task; in fact she did not outwardly acknowledge the question in any way, but a clear image appeared in Marsha's mind. The image was of an Explorer, presumably Dadive's mother, Toriol, wearing something around her neck. There was a cord there, of some smooth black material, and hanging from it was what looked to be a small nut, like an acorn, but made of glass. Marsha got the impression that it wasn't glass, not anything like it in fact, but that like a small glass vial it held a substance, a very important substance, an irreplaceable substance, and that was what the search was for. Marsha took a deep breath before asking, again as innocently and without emotion as she could muster, "What about the other Explorer, Toriol's companion? Where is he?"

Dadive looked up this time, and paused, as if she hadn't really considered where the other Explorer might be. She closed her eyes, slowly drawing the lids down over the large black pupils. Marsha thought it looked as though Dadive was listening for something, and Marsha supposed that she was probably trying to listen for the other Explorer's thoughts. Slowly Dadive opened her eyes again and looked straight at Marsha before replying flatly, "Dead."

Marsha felt instantly sad about the loss, even though these cold creatures did not seem to feel or at least did not display any sorrow or affection. "Do you know how it happened, Dadive?" she asked out loud, still trying to sound cool.

Dadive replied in the form of a question. "Crash or cat, what does it matter? The Explorers of the first pouch are gone." Dadive gestured with her long index finger toward the burnt area where the first space pouch had landed. "See human, the pouch is fading; there is no need for it. The occupants are gone; there is no way to bring them back. It is up to us to complete the mission. We must find the agent and succeed."

Shawn jumped up from where he sat on the ground and looked over to where the space pouch had crashed. "Wow, Philo, look, the pouch, it's becoming transparent! Dadive says it is fading. Let's go look!"

Marsha watched the two of them go, each digging camera phones out of their pockets, and she turned back to Dadive, who was continuing her search. "But why?" Marsha asked the Explorer. "Why have you come here? This agent, this substance that you are searching for... it is the stuff that caused your ancestors to 'become' back on Grendille? And now you want to find your ancestors here on Earth and awaken them in the same way? Why?"

"We are becoming few," was all Dadive said before the shutter came down once again.

***

182

The sleek wild cat with its tawny coat and powerful legs had a thought. "I am hungry," she said to herself, not in so many words but in something more like words than the creature had ever thought before. It was a new directive, as though the response to her natural state of hunger could suddenly be a choice, an activity that she could engage in because she wished to feel the pleasure of the flavors in her mouth and the fullness in her belly. She did not think this thought purely in reaction to her biological need, she also thought about the strange creature that she had grasped around the neck and shaken and bitten and tasted its blood and flesh. "It was good," she thought, "I want more." And so she set off back in the direction of where she had tasted the wonderful and exotic flavor of Dadive's mother, Toriol.

***

Marsha waited once more until the searching Explorers were beyond what she imagined was the telepathic reach of her thoughts. Since Marsha had sensed that Dadive had lowered the shutter that cut off communication, Marsha wasn't even sure if Dadive could hear her anyway. Maybe the telepathy between them was necessarily a two way street. Everything about the Explorers and their mission was becoming increasingly alarming to her, and she felt that she needed to talk privately with her father and work this thing out. Marsha felt danger, felt real imminent danger. Was it coming from the Explorers, from this agent that they were seeking? Or was it from somewhere else? Was it possible that she was just making it up? Marsha felt as though she couldn't trust herself to think straight, especially since she also seemed capable of communicating telepathically with Shawn. "Having other people's thoughts enter right into my brain is weird. Why in the world does it have to include Shawn's thoughts?" Marsha thought with a shudder. "I can't trust what I'm thinking. I really need to talk to Dad."

Marsha could see Philo and Shawn over by the pouch, snapping pictures of the interior of the small space vehicle by holding their newly recharged cell phone inside the hatch and pressing the shutter button, then taking it out again and reviewing the pictures in amazed delight. The pouch was becoming more and more transparent; indeed it was fading away, as Dadive had said. Apparently the thing shared some connection with its occupants and since they were no longer alive, the pouch itself had no reason to exist. Shawn and Philo were trying to capture its image on their camera before it vanished entirely.

Marsha could also see Frank, resting some distance away across the clearing; apparently he had managed to fall asleep in spite of the excitement of the cougar attack, possibly as a result of the early morning hike and the midday meal. He was leaning up against a pine tree, using a rolled up sweatshirt as a pillow. His eyes were closed, so Marsha approached quietly and whispered, "Dad, you awake?" as she sat on the ground beside him.

"Hmmm," came the grunted reply, followed by a yawn and a stretch, as Frank opened his eyes and looked at his eldest child. "What's up, Marsha? Oh, I really do love a plein air nap after lunch." He blinked the sleep away from his eyes and looked at Marsha's face. "Oh dear, you're troubled, aren't you? Upset about Toriol?"

"Dad," Marsha began timidly, "That's not it. Although that was horrible." She paused for a moment and continued. "I hope you'll tell me that I'm jumping to conclusions, or that my brain is still addled from that search beacon or from being invaded by Shawn's thoughts, but I'm confused. And worried." She brushed the dirt and pine needles from her palms and added, "Mostly worried."

Frank shifted up to a seated position and leaning forward he held his arm out. "C'mon daughter, tell me what's up," he said as he put his arm around her shoulder and she settled in next to him.

Marsha had a hard time getting started. She was known in the family as the alarmist, the worrier. Shawn often teased her about being more mom than Mom. "She's the nag, you're the worrier," he would say, to which Mom replied, "Well, if you would do all the things you're supposed to, I wouldn't have to nag, and Marsha wouldn't have to worry!" Both Shawn and Frank would roll their eyes at that one. "I...I...I, um, I sense danger, Dad," she said at last.

Frank didn't try to calm her with messages of "it'll be okay" or "you're just imagining things." This time, Frank looked at his daughter with honest and serious concern showing on his face. "Hey, tell me what you're thinking…"

"I know you guys always think I worry too much, and I'm not even really sure of why I'm feeling this way… I mean, maybe I do know why. First we wander around this forest in a daze and can't trust our own brains, and then we find this weird space nut and little alien passengers and of course then there's the telepathy thing… I mean, c'mon, can I trust my feelings? Is my brain just bruised and stretched to the limit and making stuff up?" Marsha looked at her hands and then up at her brother and cousin, still excitedly examining the disappearing space pouch. "Okay, here goes. I'm sensing danger and I think that if Dadive finds what she's looking for, this stuff that she wants to use to make the Earth's tarsiers 'become', you know, become sentient beings, that this stuff will harm people. Like it did to the people of her original planet."

"What, Grendille? You think that the stuff that made the Explorers 'become', to use their phrase, was what killed all the people on the planet?" Frank frowned and thought for a moment. "Look honey, I'm not saying that things aren't weird, but those people, well, they might not have been people. I mean, they might not have been anything like us, like Earth people. And didn't she say that they had poisoned their planet? Isn't that why they looking for another place to colonize? Maybe they destroyed their own selves. If they were capable of killing a whole planet's ecosystem, then maybe they were responsible for killing their own race."

186

Marsha looked up into her father's face. "I'd like to think you're right, Dad. Like I said, I may be jumping to conclusions, but I think this stuff could be dangerous. And, I dunno, there's something else. Something…" Marsha got up on one knee and dusted off the seat of her jeans, only to fall back down hard onto the ground.

Frank was about to laugh at Marsha's unceremonious tumble until he saw the look on her face. Marsha's eyes were open wide. They were looking in Frank's direction, staring straight at him, but Frank could tell that she didn't see him. "Marsha! Marsha? Are you alright?"

Frank's outburst startled Shawn and Philo and the pair came running from the still fading pouch. As Shawn neared where his father and sister were sitting, he stopped dead in his tracks and an odd faraway look came over his face as he stammered, "It's here, it's here, it's here…"

8 Cougar

The cat looked down on the scene below with a kind of interest that she had never before experienced. This was her third summer hunting on her own in this area since she had been sent out by her mother to fend for herself. She had learned the skills that her mother had taught her well. Not because she was a particularly clever animal, but because the skills were necessary for survival. If she hadn't learned how to be an effective hunter, she would have starved long ago. She always knew it best to wait for the cover of darkness. She knew the advantage was hers at night with her keen eye sight and alertness. But this time the wait was different. Her interest was heightened. She was anticipating events that were yet to come; anticipating the events that darkness would bring. Now, in the heat of the waning afternoon, the big cat found herself to be somewhat sleepy as she gazed from her perch at the creatures below.

There were two kinds of animal down there. Four of the creatures had very strange fur and walked on two legs. "Have I ever seen these kinds of animals before?" she wondered to herself. Her memory of the events that occurred before this afternoon was different. Her motivation used to be about one thing only: survival. The information that she registered and stored had been solely about that objective. Although she could not be sure whether or not she had seen those two-legged animals before, she had the feeling that she was supposed to avoid them. She could not at this moment figure out why. But the other, smaller, furrier animals! Now those she definitely knew! There was but one way to describe them. Mouth wateringly delicious. The cougar laid her head on her front paws as she stretched out on her high perch in preparation for a nice nap. She ran her rough tongue over her sharp teeth and dreamed of the kill to come.

***

"Marsha, are you okay?" asked Philo. He was kneeling next to his cousin and holding his camera phone, concerned for her health and yet wanting to show her the images he had taken of the fading pouch. His cousin blinked up and him and struggled to sit up on the ground beneath the leafy oak tree. "Marsha?"

"Wha- wha? Oh, Philo, it's you. Shawn... Uh, what's up? Ah, um, I guess I dozed off," she said, sleepily rubbing a few pine needles from the side of her face.

"Yeah, I guess you did. You sounded like you were purring!" her brother said, laughing. "Having a good dream? About a saucer of milk?" He chuckled again. "We wanted to show you the pictures we took. It's gone now. I mean, the pouch has vanished! Totally!"

Marsha sat up and frowned. Had she been dreaming? She felt very strange. Maybe it had been just a dream. She looked up at the late afternoon sunlight filtering down through the trees. "Uh, ah, yeah," she said looking over to where the pouch had been. "Yeah, I see. It *is* gone. That's weird. And I think I was dreaming. About being a cat. Not about a saucer of milk, I mean, not about being a house cat. But it didn't feel like a dream. It felt so real…" Marsha's voice trailed off as she looked up into the trees again.

"Ah, you're awake," said Frank, ambling over. "I think you really needed some sleep; you sure looked tired. Really, I think we all need to get back to civilization soon. This trip was supposed to be relaxing. But you both looked so strange. I think the strain of translating telepathic messages from space aliens is wearing you both out. The stress is especially showing on you, my daughter. We were just talking after lunch and then you suddenly looked so odd, Marsha. You just stopped and stared. And then Shawn ran over and then he looked weird as well." Frank looked at his son with some concern. "You were mumbling something. 'It's here' or something like that. And then Marsha, you just conked out, so I tucked my roll mat under you and let you sleep. You looked totally peaceful sleeping on

190

there on the ground. It was really sweet. You were like a cat stretched out in a sunbeam."

"That is sooo funny," said Shawn. "When we came over to show Marsha the pictures, I could've sworn she was purring! And Marsha was about to tell me about some weird dream she had about collecting Hello Kitty knick-knacks or something."

All the while her father and brother were talking about her and her little cat-nap, Marsha was looking down at the ground and frowning. She couldn't figure it out. It felt so weird, so real. Not like she had been *dreaming* of being a cat, but like she had actually been one. As though she had been thinking like a cat, thinking like a big feline hunter. "But…" she had started to say that she had been dreaming of the taste of raw meat. The delicious flavor of warm blood running down her throat. The way the little animal had tasted. Marsha was disgusted. She could almost believe that she had bitten the Explorer, had tasted its flesh and swallowed its blood. Suddenly, Marsha realized why her dream seemed so real. "Oh my gosh!" she exclaimed, "The vial, the vial! Have they found it?" She turned her face up to Frank and Shawn and then looked around for the Explorers. "I- I- I know what happened to the vial!"

***

Shawn translated what he felt to be Dadive's reaction to Marsha's news in one word: "stupid." It was the best way he could translate the derision in the Explorer's thought-message.

Marsha told the space traveler that she had received the thoughts of the mountain lion that had attacked Dadive's mother, and the only conclusion was that the predator had somehow ingested the vial containing the transformative substance and had "become" in much the same way as Dadive's ancestors. Marsha thought that the words "ridiculous" and "absurd" put Dadive's reaction into more intelligent language, but her assessment of Dadive's opinion of what she said was certainly the same.

Dadive's next thought-message took on a superior tone as she explained, "If the creature has indeed 'become' by swallowing the vial and it has spoken to you or you have accidentally listened in on its thoughts, then I certainly would have known about it."

Marsha was tired of the attitude of this little space alien. She had initially been wary of the creature's cold indifference and then had become frightened by the idea that Dadive may be in some way, intentionally or accidentally, malicious. Now Marsha found the cute appearance and superior attitude of the animal to be reminiscent of some of the stuck-up girls at school and she just wanted to be rid of her. "Fine. Whatever. Look Dadive, we've been trying to help. But I'm done now. The vial is either inside a mountain lion, or it has been broken and released into the atmosphere. In either event, there is an intelligent predator around that seems to like the way your kind tastes. We came on this trip to search for a Lingerling, but, well... Our mission here is over. *Your* mission here is over." Marsha was starting to feel increasing animosity toward Dadive and she was getting tired of this whole trip. "Look, I am done with you. There's nothing more you can do. Don't believe me, okay, but your mission really is over and your pouch may be useless. How will you get home? Is your pouch repairing itself? Is there a ship still waiting somewhere out there for you? You and Wralis might very well be stuck here in Texas, but I want to go home and have a shower. Dad, how 'bout it? I for one say it's time to pack it up and move it out. To use a Shawn-ism, it's time to split this popsicle stand."

9 Night

She awoke when the air was cool and the night sky was nearly black. The moon was just a tiny sliver, offering only the smallest bit of light. It was the kind of night which would offer the cougar many advantages and she looked down from her perch, pleased to see that the delicious prey was still nearby. "Soon," she told herself, "Soon, the feast will begin."

***

Shawn, Philo and Frank lay in the larger of the two tents, parallel to one another, each in his own sleeping bag, each completely asleep. Frank had reached a decision. This would be their last night in east Texas. In the morning they would be packing up and heading back to New Mexico. Frank was hoping for some better sort of resolution to the situation with the Explorers, but since they were stranded here on Earth, apparently without the vial of the awakening agent, their mission was at an end. Dadive had let them know that the vial contained the last remnants of the serum, and without it, they were useless. That's how Marsha received her message, not just that the mission was at an end, but that their lives were. They had no purpose, no reason to exist. The survival of their species had depended on them coming to Earth and finding the Lingerlings, but since they now had no way of awakening them, even that directive was pointless.

Marsha knew that the vial had been swallowed by the same cougar that killed Toriol. She knew that the awakening agent had been ingested along with part of the Explorer's neck. Dadive scoffed at the idea that Marsha was receiving messages from the mountain lion because she herself heard nothing. Dadive believed that perhaps the vial had been destroyed, that the fluid had been somehow spilled without causing harm to the humans or raising the awareness of the cougar. If Marsha didn't know better, she would have thought that perhaps Dadive was actually expressing an emotional response to the end of the mission, anger and resentment as a result of loss or sadness or disappointment.

Dadive thought it unlikely that the ship would still be waiting or that another pouch would be sent. That of course meant that they would be stranded here. She and Wralis had declined the invitation to return with the humans to their home, preferring to stay here in Texas, hoping that the vial could still, somehow, be retrieved.

Frank told the Explorers about the Earth primates called tarsiers, and how like them they were and he offered to somehow get them to the Philippines or somewhere where they could find a population of the Explorer-like creatures and live out their days on this alien planet. The idea seemed to horrify Dadive, as though he had suggested that she and Wralis move in with a family of backward ruffians.

Marsha lay awake, alone in her little tent, staring up into the darkness. The night was clear; no chance of rain, so the fly cover was left off of the tent and the little screened vent at the very top afforded a beautiful view of the stars. If Marsha saw them, she was not aware. Neither was she aware of the cool of the air, the fragrant smell of the pines, nor the sounds of the night insects and frogs. Once again, in her mind, she was being transported up into the branches. Once again she was feeling decidedly feline. Once again she could remember the taste of the delicious warm flesh of the little space Explorer.

***

The cat pondered her memory for the first time. Indeed, it was the first time that she realized that she *had* such a place inside herself where information could be retained and drawn on at will. Her memory told her that she had bitten down into the neck of the odd little creature and it was delicious. Then suddenly it wasn't quite so delicious and then she "became." She remembered this. Plus, she remembered how she felt before. Before, it was all about the survival. She remembered that she had tasted a creature like that once before, but she did not register that it was anything other than sustenance. This second meal she did not get to finish. And she wanted more. Those other animals, the ones with two legs, had chased her away. They had waved something at her and she had been afraid. But why? "Their sticks are no match for my teeth and claws," she thought. "I will not be afraid of them this time. There are more of those delicious little animals down below, and I will have them." She purred to herself and thought some more. "Hmm, and maybe I will taste and see if the two-legged creatures are delicious as well."

***

While the cat was thinking these things up in the branches of the oak tree, Marsha was thinking these things as well, tucked all the way down into her sleeping bag. Suddenly, as if waking from a dream, she became aware of the thoughts inside her head and she was frightened. "I am not making this up!" she said into the darkness of the tent. "Dad! Shawn! Philo! Get up! There is a mountain lion here somewhere and she is going to attack!" Marsha scrambled out of her sleeping bag and ran towards the tent where the others were sleeping. "Dad, get up!" Marsha did not see the Explorers, did not know where they were spending the night, but she was not particularly worried about them. "Dad!"

Frank stuck his head out of the tent flap. "What is it, Marsha? Where's the fire?"

197

"No fire, Dad, but a cougar. I know it's nearby. I know it's thinking of attacking. It's even wondering how we'd taste!" Marsha pulled on her father's arm, trying to drag him out of the tent. "Wake the guys, we've got to go; we've got to get to safety!"

Frank complied, noting instantly how upset his daughter was. Even if there wasn't actually a lion in the vicinity, his daughter's agitated state needed immediate attention. "Okay, okay, Shawn, Philo, Marsha says it's time to go. C'mon guys, grab your flashlights, leave the stuff, just leave it. Let's get a move on."

Shawn was making the usual grunting noises that always accompanied his waking up, while Philo was stammering, "Wha? Wha?" when suddenly a horrible scream pierced the night.

"Wralis!" exclaimed Marsha, hearing the scream with both her ears and her mind. "Oh no! She got Wralis!"

"Whaddya mean, 'she got Wralis'?" exclaimed Philo. "Who did? What was that awful sound?" They were all piling out of the tent now, with Frank holding his flashlight and looking around with the weak beam into the darkness. The two teen-aged boys began ransacking their packs, feeling for flashlights, and wondering what the heck was going on.

"Marsha says there's a mountain lion out there and that it's got Wralis," said Frank, quickly trying to explain the situation to the boys.

"How do you know it's a mountain lion? You're not claiming to read its mind again is you?" laughed Shawn, but only half-heartedly, because he had felt it too, just a flash, much less intensely than Marsha, maybe because he felt it second-hand, through Marsha.

A horrible scream pierced the darkness once more, this time sounding fainter and weaker than before. "Yes, I am," stated Marsha. "I can hear the cougar's thoughts." She hung her head for a moment. "She has just killed Wralis. She's eating his body, and… and… no, it's too horrible…" Marsha stopped speaking for a moment and put her hands over her mouth. "Dadive," she whispered through her fingers, "Where's Dadive?"

Shawn's hand finally grasped his flash light and he flicked it on as he pulled it out of his pack. He shone it near his sister and they could all see the look on her face. "Hey, she's not kidding!" said Philo.

"No, I'm not. The cougar swallowed the vial. Like I said! I heard her thinking about it. In my head. The cougar was thinking about how Toriol… about how Dadive's mother… well, she was thinking about how she, um, tasted… it was good and then suddenly something tasted bad and then the cougar 'became'. She spoke of it just like the Explorers had spoken about it. And now she's hungry. She's hungry for more."

Shawn shouted uselessly off into the darkness, "Dadive!" He wanted to warn the creature about the imminent danger. Of course, the space traveler already knew the fate of Wralis, her mate. Plus, she knew the cause.

Frank shook his head as he whispered hurriedly to the three teens in his care, "Go! Now! All of you. That way. I want you to go. Put as much distance as possible between yourselves and the cougar. I'll see if I can help Dadive while the cat is eating." Marsha, Shawn and Philo hesitated until Frank shouted, "Look, would you go already! Go! You've got the flashlights! I'll be right behind you! Promise."

"But Dad, you've got no weapon!" exclaimed Marsha. "You can't fight a lion!"

"Don't worry. I do know a little something about their behavior. Give your old dad some credit and go!"

"But Dad, this is no ordinary mountain lion!" argued Marsha. "This lion can think!"

"But I'm your father. And I say go!" said Frank, with a tone of uncharacteristic severity.

Reluctantly, the three teens took off in the direction that Frank had indicated. They had two flashlights between them, and were sticking close together in an effort to steer clear of the trees and bushes that appeared up out of the darkness as they hurried away.

They had gone about two hundred yards when Marsha suddenly stopped dead in her tracks and covered her face with her hands, causing Philo to crash into the back of her. "Oh no!" she cried, "The cougar! Look out! Dadive!"

"What? What is it?" asked Philo in a rush. "What's happening?"

Shawn spoke, breathing hard from running. "Dadive sees the cat. It's stalking her. She knows it is about to attack. She wants us all to run! Dadive wants us to leave her. She says we are to save ourselves and run! Her message is to save ourselves..."

"She is, she is, she's telling us to get away. Dadive is actually thinking about us." Marsha took on the posture and expression of heartbreak, in disbelief that all this time she had thought that Dadive was without empathy. Maybe she had misjudged her. But suddenly Marsha realized where her father was. "Dad! Dad! Run, you can't save Dadive, she doesn't want you to. She wants you to save yourself. Run!" In spite of her father's firm instructions, Marsha grabbed the flashlight from Shawn and ran back in the direction of Frank, of Dadive, and of the hungry cougar.

"No, Marsha! Dad said to go this way! You..." Shawn shouted uselessly into the dark as Marsha's flashlight beam got dimmer and further away.

10 The Kill

Frank could see the eyes of the big cat glowing from out of the darkness as the animal prepared to pounce. The cougar's gaze was not directed at Frank, and suddenly he was able to make out the cat's intended target. The Explorer Dadive was simply standing there motionless. She did not appear to be frozen with fear; instead, she appeared to simply be waiting for what was about to happen with the calm patience of someone waiting for a bus. And then it did happen. The mountain lion pounced on the tiny creature; the creature who had travelled so far, only to die in this east Texas forest. Frank turned away. He couldn't bear to watch as the cougar tore into Dadive. Even though Frank had witnessed countless such kills during his career as a zoologist, this of course was different. He felt a tremendous sadness. He was devastated at witnessing the horror of the vicious and bloody attack, but more than that, he was sorrowful about the attitude of the little Explorer. She gave herself up to the cougar instead of trying to escape, instead of trying to live. Apparently Dadive had felt that because her mission was a failure, her purpose had expired and her life should expire too. Frank stood there dumbly, only half thinking that he should run, or climb, or find a large rock, or something, when he heard the sound of someone running through the underbrush. The sound of leaves and twigs snapping and crunching grew louder, and finally he heard the sound of his daughter's voice, calling, "Dad!"

"No!" Frank shouted, waving his arms wildly, "No!"

In her mind, Marsha could no longer hear Dadive. She knew the little space traveler was no longer alive. She felt an odd hollow despair at the creature's demise, but more urgently, she could still hear her father calling, telling her to go away, to get away, to run. Alarmingly, she could hear the cougar too. The big cat's brain was in overdrive, the excitement of the kill making her want more. The cougar was wondering what the two legged animal would taste like; Marsha could hear the animal as she pondered what Marsha's own father would taste like!

"No!" Frank shouted again into the darkness. "Go! I told you to go!" Frank turned back to the grisly scene and saw that the cougar had turned her attention from the bloody mess that was once Dadive to Frank himself. Again Frank shouted, "Nooo!" as he finally turned to run. The mountain lion, all claws and teeth and powerful sinewy muscles was prepared to pounce once more. The beast growled a snarling guttural sound and although she usually preferred to leap onto her prey from a position of height, the big cat had no choice but to launch her body from where she stood on the ground. Her strong muscles tensed and released in a powerful motion and she landed, claws extended, onto Frank's back just as a shot rang out from the darkness. Both Frank and the mountain lion collapsed together in a tangled heap on the forest floor.

***

The dawn came up as usual and the group's spirits were a confusion of low and high, a jumble of sorrow and rejoicing in regards to the events of the previous night. Certainly Frank, Marsha, Shawn and Philo couldn't be happier that Mr. Shepherd had come along just when he did. As they all sat around Mr. Shepherd's campsite, the man explained how he had gone on this trip with his two grandkids, hoping to show them the Lingering, the living fossil that he had discovered. It was the single skillful shot from his rifle that had ended the life of the cougar but had saved the life of Shawn and Marsha's father. Frank smiled broadly as he said, "You'll never know just how grateful we are that you happened along with that rifle, Mr. Shepherd!"

"Oh, call me Chuck, please," he said, turning pancakes in an aluminum pan on a tiny propane stove. "I sure was glad that we were out here; glad I was there to help. Now don't you folks go telling Jorge, that old so-and-so park ranger. Hunting season is over and we're not supposed to be out here without a back country permit. That feller's always so bossy. Nosy, too."

"If hunting season is over, then why *did* you bring the rifle, Mr. Shepherd?" asked Shawn. "On the lookout for Bigfoot are you?"

"Ha, did Jorge tell you that one? What an old gossip. Nah, I tell him those Bigfoot stories just to keep him and the other rangers entertained. Ain't no such thing. No, I just brung the gun fer rattlesnakes. They get pretty frisky at this time of year. Didn't bring it for Bigfoots, nor Loch Ness Monsters, or aliens, and apparently I didn't bring it fer no Lingerlings neither."

Marsha had bandaged the scratches on her father's back as best she could. Although his sweatshirt was in tatters, his back would heal. Only one of the scratches looked like it might need stitches, and certainly some antibiotics, but that could wait. Frank looked around at each of the three teenagers sitting comfortably near. "Nope, apparently no Lingerlings," he said. "At least, we never found any. But listen Mr. Shepherd, ah, Chuck, I mean, I'm gonna give you my card and you keep your eyes peeled. Let me know if you see any more of them, okay? Or if you see any strange plants, either. Hmm, say, like, I dunno, any giant nuts or anything," he added casually.

"Giant nuts? Ha, sure thing, Frank." Mr. Shepherd smiled amiably. "Now, any of you want some more bacon or pancakes? There's plenty."

Shawn was the first to speak up. "I can't believe I'm sayin' this, but no thanks Mr. Shepherd! I'm stuffed!" Shawn gave a broad smile and added, "I sure do like the way that you camp!"

***

Standing in a circle, Frank and the kids were surveying the tragic scene. They each had their pack on their back and were looking forward to getting out of this forest, getting out of Texas, and going back home. "So what do we do, Dad? Do we need to bring back, um, anything?" asked Marsha. She looked down at the dead mountain lion, a truly beautiful animal, and though she felt sad, she could also feel something else, something that she did not want to acknowledge. Marsha was sure that she could still hear her brother. Even though the Explorers and their telepathic abilities were gone, she could still hear Shawn. He was about to speak, and she knew what he was going to say.

"Like what, Sis?" he asked her. "Not much left. I mean, not much left of the Explorers."

Philo spoke up. "I guess the other space pouch must be gone, too," he said sadly.

"Yes, well, there is also this mountain lion," said Marsha. "It may have the vial inside of it. Or at least the stuff that was in the vial." She thought it possible that some of Dadive and Wralis was inside the lion as well.

"You could do an autopsy, Dad," said Shawn, echoing the thoughts that Marsha did not want to say out loud. Marsha looked at her father, hoping he would say no to the idea. Then she looked at Shawn. Could he still hear her thoughts too? She was unhappily certain that she could still hear him.

"Well, I am a little bit concerned about what could happen if another animal were to eat the flesh of this cougar... But I'm not even sure what to think about that. What could happen if an ant or beetle or vulture or coyote were to snack on this cougar and 'become'? I don't know. No, I think what we should do is let the park rangers know that there was an accident and let them dispose of the body. We'll call 'em just as soon as we get back to the truck." Frank paused and added. "I don't think it's a good idea to mention any of the other stuff. We'll just let Ranger Jorge or whoever know that we were being attacked by this mountain lion and lucky for us, Mr. Shepherd stepped in and saved the day. Keep it simple."

The four of them, each with a sorrowful look on his or her face, gazed at the carcass of the cougar for a few moments before one by one, they all turned and walked away, heading for the trail that would lead them to their truck.

11 Home

"Well, well, the returning heroes!" said Trudy grinning broadly. Candy was taking turns to jump up on each of them as they emerged from the pickup truck, her wet nose and lolling tongue hoping to reach all the way up to their faces. "Oh, we are so glad to have you back! Aren't we Candy? Did you guys have fun? Did you find your missing link?" Trudy hugged them each in turn, but managed not to notice when Frank winced from the scratches that still smarted on his back. Trudy attributed their quiet subdued demeanors to the long drive.

Frank looked at the others and then soberly addressed his wife. "Hi, honey. We kind of did find a missing link of sorts. Our link to the stars as it turns out. But, well, we'll tell you about it later. I've got road weariness and I'm pretty sure we could all use showers and food."

"Oh sure! You'll be glad to know that I have completely stocked the fridge! Come in, come in!" Trudy was smiling broadly and talking rapidly in her excitement at having her family return in one piece. She turned to her son and gave him a hug. "I can't believe you didn't want to stop in Roswell on the way home, Shawn! You *must* have missed your old mom!"

"Oh he missed you alright, Aunt Trudy,'" laughed Philo, hugging her tightly before ascending the stairs of the mobile home, "but I think even more than that, Shawn is just a wee bit tired of aliens!"

Trudy raised her eyebrows in honest surprise. "Tired of aliens?" she asked. "Hmm." She looked at her son, but spoke to her husband. "What did you do to my Shawn, Frank?"

"Trudy, do you remember when I talked to you on the phone and I told you about the little aliens?" asked Frank. When Trudy looked at him quizzically he continued. "You remember, I told you about how that meteor that you saw was really a space craft? Well, I wasn't fibbing. Honest I wasn't." Frank sighed as he sat down on the sofa and put his feet up on the hassock. "Trudy," he said, "if you get me a can of soda, and make sure it's cold, I'll tell you all about it."

Trudy listened politely and with some great amusement to the story Frank told, while Philo and Shawn joined in to embellish the tale with various other anecdotes and bits of information. Trudy knew a little bit about their confusion in the woods from talking to them on the phone, but she had a hard time believing what they claimed to be the cause. So Frank told Trudy about finding the weird giant nut and the creature that emerged from it and Shawn told her about the first time Dadive spoke directly into his brain. Philo excitedly revealed details about the interior of the space pouch and how parts of it were made of a strange gaseous material and parts looked to be made of living green plants. Then Shawn interrupted Philo to tell Trudy about the history of the planet Grendille and about the images that Dadive had shown him of life there. Trudy was just on the verge of telling them all that they must have had lots of fun filling the hours in the truck by coming up with this unbelievable story when Philo reached into his pocket, pulled out his phone, and showed her the pictures that he and Shawn had taken of the Explorers and their space craft.

"Oh, oh, oh, you weren't kidding!" she stammered. "I don't believe it! I can't believe it!" She put her hand to her forehead and looked up at Frank. "But, where are they now, these little aliens? You didn't bring any home?" She looked around her as if expecting some strange creature to appear from behind the sofa.

While the guys were telling Trudy the story in their animated fashion, Marsha had remained quiet and subdued, but now she spoke up, trying to explain about how worried she had been that these cute creatures could possibly cause the destruction of life here on Earth. She told her mom that she had been afraid that their mission was so narrow in focus that they didn't care what effect their serum might have had on the humans or other living creatures. In the end though, the species that was destroyed turned out to be the Explorers. Their last ditch attempt at repopulating their home planet with the ancestors left behind on Earth, whether those ancestors turned out to be an extinct omomyid or living tarsier, proved to be impossible. The serum was apparently lost, the Explorers were all killed. Sadly, Marsha finished telling Trudy the rest of the story, including the tragic ending. She concluded with the mountain lion attacks, and Frank showed Trudy the claw marks he had on his back to prove it.

What Marsha didn't say, nor did Shawn, was that there were some unusual lasting effects from their encounter with the little aliens. Shawn and Marsha were still in contact with one another telepathically, a fact that left them each a bit disgusted. Marsha felt that she finally understood a bit of the reason behind the cool demeanor of the Explorers. She thought it likely that they were just permanently annoyed at having other personalities invading their most private of spaces: their minds. Marsha was determined to figure out how to bring down that mental shutter that would end the open connection with her brother in the way that Dadive had managed to do so well.

***

Later that night, Frank and Trudy sat watching the stars from the swing out in the yard. Candy was fast asleep, lying on the ground with her head resting on Frank's feet and the three

211

teenagers were also conked out, asleep in the house after a dinner of several frozen pizzas. Trudy put her arm around Frank, taking care not to touch his wounded back, and said, "It's hard to believe, but you really were telling the truth weren't you? About the aliens? And about all the rest? Frank, you almost got killed by a mountain lion. I must do something really nice for Mr. Shepherd. I hope he's not in too much trouble for shooting that cougar. But can you do something really nice for me? Can you please not leave my sight anymore? You are always getting into trouble."

The End

Also available by Laura Wacha

THE RUMINATORS

It's been almost a year since Dad went to the store for roofing supplies and never came back. One day he was joking that he saw a supposedly mythical chupacabra in the back yard, the next day, he was gone. For Marsha, a camping trip to the remote desert mountain known as "Thieves Peak" with her younger brother and their out of town cousin could be the perfect summer distraction from the inexplicable paternal abandonment. Cousin Philo hopes to find the gold bars that locals say Wild West bandits have hidden in the rugged foothills, but Shawn just wants to scare the city dude with wild campfire tales of blood sucking monsters.

When a sinkhole opens beneath their feet, the three teens are swallowed into the midst of a colony of odd mutant creatures, and may turn out to be the unwitting snacks for a pair of real life chupacabras that are loose in the old mining tunnels. Could it be that the sudden and mysterious disappearance of Shawn and Marsha's father actually had something to do with all of this?

This sci-fi adventure for YA audiences is laced with smart facts, strange fantasies and wild conspiracy theories about the natural environment and nuclear history of high desert New Mexico.